Where the Turnpike Starts

by Harriett H. Carr

WHERE THE TURNPIKE STARTS

The Macmillan Company
new york, 1955

To Lavinia Dobler

Where the Turnpike Starts

Boy Governor of Michigan

It was late May, but a chill wind from the lakes rippled the leaves of the Normandy pear trees and fanned the white arms of the old windmills that lined the main street of Detroit. In all her fifteen years, Anne Rogers had never seen such windmills. Made of timber they were, with the lower story filled in, and encased in stone. She took note of them as she hurried along. They must have been built one hundred years ago. In 1735 perhaps, by the old French settlers who came to Michigan in the days of Cadillac.

"Northwest corner of Woodbridge and Randolph Streets," she repeated to herself. From the upper deck of the steamer the Captain had pointed the location out to her and she had promised her father she would take the letter of introduction to the hotel for him. Papa had enough to do, looking out for the animals and all that great load of household goods his young wife had brought with her from Boston way.

Anne turned the corner. A wild gust of wind twisted her large, flaring bonnet from its insecure perch atop a knot of heavy brown hair. One hand to her hat, the other to the flounces of her blue cashmere morning dress, and the letter sailed off across the narrow, ribbon-like farms that stretched to the north of the street.

"Oh!" It was almost a sob. She couldn't lose that letter! She couldn't go back and tell Papa it had blown away. Not in front of his new wife. She tried to follow the speck of white, but before she had gone more than a step or two it disappeared beyond clusters of the strange pear trees that were everywhere about the place.

"Oh, no!" She swallowed hard to keep back the tears.

"Was it a tremendously important letter?"

Startled, Anne turned back to the street. The girl who had spoken was older than she. Eighteen or nineteen, perhaps.

"It was terribly important," Anne told her. "I know what it said but I can't remember the name of the man I was taking it to."

"I'll help you if I can," the girl promised. "You just came in on one of the steamers, didn't you?"

Anne nodded. "How did you know?"

"I live here. I know most of the people I see on the street. My name is Susan Williams."

Anne introduced herself. Susan was not as tall as she, but Anne was tall for her age, she knew. Such a pretty girl, Anne thought; light curls and pleasant, rounding features, and hazel eyes that just looked at you but didn't seem to say anything.

"I was taking a letter to a man who runs a hotel here, so he'll get rooms ready for us," Anne explained. "You see, there're a lot of us. My Papa, Martin Rogers and his wife. And Aunt Ellen Crawford and her husband Luther Crawford, and my cousin Nate and the little Crawford cousins, and me." The words tumbled out.

Susan Williams shook her head. "You couldn't get a room in any hotel or tavern or anywhere else in Detroit. Not if the letter was from President Jackson himself," she said.

"Why not?"

"Because of the Constitutional Convention. Didn't you know?"

Anne hadn't known.

"All the important men in Michigan are here in the capital," Susan told her. "They're helping our wonderful Boy Governor write a constitution so we can become a state. You'll just have to stay on the boat. That's what all the emigrants do."

But Anne wasn't convinced.

"If I could only remember the man's name," she said. "I'd go and tell him what happened, and how Papa got the letter back in Connecticut. It was from a man who knows them both. A man who manufactures clocks. I've just got to remember."

"I know all the hotels," Susan said dubiously. "There's the Mansion House. . . ."

"It's at the northeast corner of Woodbridge and Randolph," Anne said hopefully.

-3-

"That's the Steamboat Hotel. It's run by 'Uncle Ben' Woodworth. Is that the name?"

Anne's long sigh of relief was answer enough. The distressed look vanished and her blue eyes danced as she smiled at Susan.

"You just don't know how relieved I am," she said. "I simply couldn't go back to the boat and admit I'd lost that letter."

"But you're going to talk to a man you don't even know?" Susan questioned.

Anne looked away. "I don't mind," she said. "I can tell him all about us and if he really hasn't any place for us, I can tell Papa what he said. It's not that I'm afraid to tell Papa about the letter," she added hastily. "It's — another reason."

Susan did not press for an answer, although plainly she did not understand Anne's reasoning. With a bit of a shrug she pointed the way to the hotel.

"I'll see you again I hope," she said pleasantly. "Maybe I'll see you at the circus. There's a circus in town and everybody'll be there, you know. Only you wouldn't know, of course."

"No," Anne admitted, "but if there's a circus, probably we'll go. Where is it to be found?"

"Out on the common, near the capitol building," Susan said and pointed to the north. "Sometimes we call it Capital Park."

"I imagine Papa'll take me. Likely to the capitol building too. Papa's a great one for getting about and seeing everything," Anne said proudly.

—4—

"Then probably I will see you again. Good bye for now," Susan answered.

Anne had no trouble finding the Steamboat Hotel, nor in seeing Uncle Ben Woodworth, but it was just as Susan had said. There were no rooms to be had. From the noisy, talkative men who lounged about, she learned that indeed there wasn't a room to be had in Detroit. For weeks people had been coming to Michigan from New York and Massachusetts and all the eastern states. Now the Constitutional Convention had crowded the city with more people.

The hotel buzzed with excitement. "It's been like this ever since the Erie Canal opened in 1826, you might say," Uncle Ben told her. "Why, one day last October nine hundred passengers landed here. One day, mind you. October 7th, 'twas."

"This summer bids fair to beat all for emigration," a clerk at the desk chimed in. "Three thousand boats are operating on the Erie Canal, and seventy-five lake steamers have docked here already this month."

"Passage is cheap, too," an onlooker chimed in. "Twenty-two dollars and fifty-two cents, Albany to Detroit. Freight is only thirty-eight cents a hundredweight for heavy goods and fifty cents for light goods and furniture."

"Cheap and easy," Uncle Ben continued, smiling at Anne. "You folks from back east can get a canal boat out of Albany for Buffalo every hour. Three or four days on the Canal, then forty hours on a Lake Erie steamer, and here you be! Small wonder the emigrant tide has left the

Cumberland Road for Ohio to take the water route to Michigan."

All this Anne knew. "What do they do when they get here?" she finally asked a little impatiently. "Where do they stay, I mean?"

"Do? They move inland along the Chicago Turnpike, mainly," Uncle Ben replied. "Right now they stay on the steamer while they get loaded and ready to push on. The steamers always put up here one night, at least."

So the letter would have done no good, even if she had it. Slowly she walked back to the river landing with her disappointing answer.

At the dock she surveyed the boat thoroughly, hoping to see her father, or even Cousin Nate, but neither was in sight. Carefully she picked her way about the lower deck where horses and wagons, farm tools and household goods were piled to the ceiling. They were not there. Nor did a turn about the upper deck meet with success. Reluctantly she went to her father's cabin. At the door she hesitated and listened.

Anne felt tight inside whenever she was alone with her stepmother. If there were other people about, it wasn't so bad. When Papa was there, with his gaiety and laughter and singing, she could nearly forget that Polly was his wife. It was almost like the years after Mama had died, when there was only Papa and Granny and herself, Anne. But when she was alone with Polly, Anne's throat got tense and her stomach too, and there was a tight feeling around her heart. She never knew what to say, and sometimes she had to clear her throat before she could speak at all. So now she listened, hoping to hear voices and be assured that someone — anyone at all — was inside with Polly. But there were no sounds and at last she knocked lightly, then opened the door and peered in.

Polly Rogers was the prettiest woman Anne had ever seen. Tiny and feminine she was, with chestnut hair and large brown eyes, and a quietness about her that Anne did not understand. There was determination behind her air of composure and many little things that happened now were Polly's idea. Like the grown-up way Anne was wearing her hair, and the big, stylish bonnet made like a picture in Godey's "Lady's Book." Lately Polly had been talking about how becoming curls were for young ladies, and Anne's brown locks were straight as a string. So that meant doing her hair up on rags every night.

Granny had said Polly came from an aristocratic family and was real well-bred, and Papa always spoke about Polly's folks in a slow sort of voice. Maybe Papa wasn't actually afraid of Polly's brother Eb, but that was the way it sounded to Anne whenever Eb's name was mentioned. It made Anne hurt inside. It wasn't like a Yankee peddler to be afraid of anything.

Anne stood in the doorway for a moment, watching while Polly carefully packed her dresses, placing paper between each fold. They would all have to be gone over with a sadiron before they could be worn, so why was she fussing so?

Anne cleared her throat. "Polly, Ma'am," she apologized. Never could she call anyone so young "Mama."

"Oh, Anne! You startled me."

"I didn't mean to. I — I just wondered where Papa was."

"He's with the Captain, I think. I haven't seen him since you left," Polly replied. "What did you find out at the hotel?"

It was like Polly to ask about the errand right away, without waiting for Anne to tell Papa how she had made out. 'Twas he who had sent her on the errand. Granny would have gone on about her business and left Anne to tell Papa first. But Granny had gone to live with Aunt Mercy where there were no growing girls to try her patience, and here was she, Anne, on her way to a new home somewhere in Michigan with Papa and his strange wife.

Anne heard his footsteps then, as he turned into the corridor and came toward the cabin. She would not need to answer Polly now. Quick, solid steps they were. He always knew where he was going and was in a hurry to get there. Another minute and there he was, handsome and smiling and fairly filling the room, for he was a heavy-set, well-built man and the cabin was small.

"Well, well, well! Back already. But without any rooms at the hotel for us, I'll warrant," and his broad, friendly hand moved in Anne's direction as though he was about to give her a genial swat. That was a way he had. He made you want him to do it.

"How did you know?" Anne asked, smiling back at him.

"No rooms at the hotel!" Polly gasped and turned from her packing to look inquiringly from Anne to Papa.

"We'll have to spend the night on the steamboat for there's not a room to be had in Detroit for love nor money," Papa went on, winking at Polly. "Beside, that's what all the emigrants do."

"Papa! How did you know?"

He laughed and his long, black lashes curled upward mischievously. Anne's lashes were like that too. It was the only thing about her whole appearance that really pleased her. Papa had waving black hair, and a moustache that he spent no end of pains keeping clipped short and neat. And a way of looking just at you, as though nobody else mattered. Small wonder all the ladies bought his clocks and umbrellas and laces and silver when he stopped his peddler's wagon at their doors.

"There's one thing I'll wager you don't know," Anne told him.

"There's a Constitutional Convention going on in Detroit," he guessed.

"That Captain must know everything, almost," Anne replied. "But there's something else."

He arched his heavy eyebrows and looked at her with mock seriousness. "You met a fellow!" he said.

"No! There's a circus in town!"

"A circus? Tease me to take you. Come on!"

Anne had been sure he would take her. She hoped that Polly would not go, so she would have a chance to be alone with Papa and tell him the truth about the letter. He looked at his wife, a little dubiously Anne thought.

"Mrs. Rogers, have you an interest in this circus?" he asked Polly. "Or are circuses just for little children?"

"Little children!" Anne protested. But she didn't really mind.

"I do think I've outgrown circuses, Mr. Rogers," Polly said. "But you two go. Perhaps Sister Ellen and I will take a short walk about town whilst you're gone."

Anne tried not to show her relief.

It was so easy to explain things to Papa. While they walked to the circus he listened to her story and nodded his head. Anne was sure he understood. Even at times when she knew in her heart that she had been in the wrong, Papa understood. But today he agreed it wasn't her fault, and that she had done right well to go to the hotel and find out about the situation for him. Before she had fairly finished telling about the men at the Steamboat Hotel, they had reached the commons. Mingling with the crowd at the circus, the letter was soon forgotten.

A clown, standing on a box, was telling jokes and blaring a trumpet to get attention. Two fiddlers scratched away at their violin strings as the clown shouted the praises of the breath-taking acts which were about to start. On either side of the entrance to the tent were the brightly-painted circus wagons. One depicted Noah and the animals on the Ark. The other displayed a muscular Samson, crumbling temple pillars in each hand. Heavy draft horses munched grass beside the wagons and there was a smell of animals about the tents.

Papa shouldered and side-stepped his way through the crowd to stand close beside the clown's box.

"Got any horses?" he asked. "Show horses I mean, not baggage horses."

The clown took up the words, calling attention to

three or four spotted ponies, bedecked with bell-trimmed harnesses.

"Our riders were trained by the great John Robinson!" he cried. "Best horses and riders on earth!"

Papa asked about the acrobats and jugglers and nodded agreement to each of the clown's exaggerations. When the crowd moved into the tent, the man stepped from his box to stand beside Papa.

"What's your line, Mister?" he asked.

"I'm a peddler," Papa told him. "How's business in Michigan?"

"No good except Detroit and maybe Monroe and Toledo way," the clown replied. "Even a mud show like mine can't get through the roads they have here."

"What about the Turnpike?" Papa asked. "I thought it was an extension of the water route, starting here and going right through to Chicago."

"Such as it is, that's where it goes," the clown replied. "Follows the old Indian trails, snakin' around swamps and peat bogs. But if you take my advice, you'll head south to Ohio. They're thirty years ahead of Michigan. Got towns and roads that don't fall out from under you. Michigan's no good for road men and won't be for another ten years."

"I know the southern states are better show states, but there's more competition for peddlers there, too," Papa reasoned.

"Wherever you go, my friend, you've got the same competition as me," the clown answered. "You've got the elements agin you. You've got poor crops and folks without money to contend with. You meet up with cholera and floods and highwaymen. But in Ohio you can at least keep movin'! Michigan? They can have it for another ten years, like I said."

Papa looked thoughtful and Anne felt disturbed.

"I don't like the sound of that," Papa said to the clown. "I'd been figuring on locating along the Turnpike somewhere. Getting a head start on the trade that's bound to be here as towns develop and the territory gets settled up."

"You've been lookin' at too many of John Farmer's maps and gazeteers, my friend," the circus man laughed a little bitterly. "Take my advice and move into Ohio. They've been a state since 1802. Got their representatives in Congress. Why, this territory's got nothin' but Pottawattomies west of Washtenaw County."

Anne watched her father as he went on questioning the clown. This was bad news, she knew. Papa had made contracts with the manufacturing firms whose merchandise he sold. Anne was sure he was expected to take their goods into Michigan. Some other peddler represented them in Ohio.

"Papa, could we change now?" Anne asked as they went into the tent.

"I don't know, Anne," Papa said thoughtfully. "All of my plans were for Michigan. Uncle Luther's, too. Land is cheap in Michigan. A farm would cost more than Uncle Luther can pay, in Ohio."

"Aren't you supposed to take your clocks and things into Michigan?" she pressed. "Didn't you say you would?"

"Yes, but now's no time to study it out," he replied. "Why don't you look for your friend, Susan? Anyway, here come the acrobats."

From time to time Anne's eyes turned from the acts that took over the one ring of the circus to her father's face. Surely he wasn't really watching, not even when a man in purple tights walked the tight rope across the length of the tent. The enthusiasm of other spectators failed to lift her spirits. Soon she, too, was staring at the ring without mirth or interest.

"That clown spoiled it for both of us, didn't he?" Papa asked quietly. "I've got another idea. Come on."

Anne didn't ask him what the idea was. Without a word she followed him out of the tent.

"The Captain told me about this Constitutional Convention they're holding," he explained. "I guess you heard about it too, didn't you?"

Anne repeated all she could remember of what Susan Williams had told her.

"Let's go over to the capitol building and see if we can pick up any news there," Papa suggested. "Maybe you'll have to go back to the boat alone. I might have to go to one of the hotels or other gathering places tonight. You don't mind, do you?"

"No," and Anne shook her head.

"Then come on. We'll see what we can find out."

A small crowd had gathered outside the building and Papa had no trouble starting a conversation.

"Good sized structure," he said to the man next to him. "What is it, 60' x 90'?"

"That's right. We built it about ten years ago," the man replied with a note of pride. "Cost $24,500."

"Two story, I see," Papa continued.

"Yep. Meeting rooms are upstairs. 'Twas used for a hospital in the first cholera epidemic."

"Has this convention been going on long?" Papa asked.

"Since May 11th," the man answered. "Our delegates are writing a constitution that'll be better'n any state in the Union's got."

"Better'n Ohio's got by far," another man chimed in. "We've got better militia, too. I wisht Gov'ner Mason had gone ahead last month and let Gen'ral Brown march 'em down there. We'd a-shown 'em who holds Toledo."

"I read something about it in the papers," Papa said. "What was it all about?"

"You from back East?"

"Just got in this morning," Papa explained.

"It's allowable that you don't rightly know, then," the first man conceded. Then everyone began explaining the trouble to Papa.

"This here Gov'ner Lucas of Ohio is tryin' to change the boundary line. Wants to take Toledo and a strip of land clean acrost the southern edge of the Territory away from us," one man explained.

"The Ohio folks is callin' the district around Toledo 'Lucas County'. They've set up what they call the 'Harris Line' an' aim to make that the boundary."

It didn't mean much to Anne and she scarcely listened at first, but it was plain that Papa was heeding every word. This might be important to him, she knew.

"Ohio's trying to keep us out of the Union, too," Anne heard an older voice explaining. "But they can't do it. When Congress adjourned in March without taking us in, our Governor acted. We're holding this Constitutional Convention here and now. We're going to be a state in spite of Ohio."

"It's the slave power that's trying to keep us out of the Union," another man chimed in. "Michigan'll be a free state. That'll swing the balance of power in the U.S. Senate away from the slave states. Press up a little closer, stranger. Maybe you can hear some of the debate that's going on inside."

Anne clung to her father's arm as he moved nearer the doorway. She could hear voices inside, but could not distinguish more than an occasional word. At last there was a hush. She looked from one man to another for an explanation.

"I think our Governor is going to speak, young lady," the older man whispered. "Stevens Thompson Mason. Only nineteen years old he was when President Jackson appointed him Secretary of the Territory, and there was bitter feeling against him. But he's turned out to be wonderful. A marvelous, smart boy. He's only twenty-three now."

The voice Anne heard next, in the stillness outside the capitol of Michigan Territory, was clear and forceful. It thrilled her with the same fervor that moved the convention delegates within and the crowd outside.

". . . Under the compact between the United States and the people of the Northwest Territory, Michigan *is of right entitled* to organize a state government and be admitted to the Union."

Anne pressed forward and stood on her tiptoes, but she could not see inside.

"We are here to write a constitution that will be republican in form. The fifth article of the Ordinance of 1787, enacted for the government of the Northwest Territory, provides that whenever any state has 60,000 free inhabitants it *shall be* admitted by its delegates into the Congress of the United States, on an equal footing with the original states in all respects whatsoever; and shall be at liberty to form a permanent constitution and state government. We are now a state with 85,856 people, larger than any territory previously admitted to statehood from the Northwest."

"Is that the Governor?" Anne whispered to her father.

"I think so. Hush!"

"We have waited long enough for Congress to pass an enabling act! We shall assume our *right* to statehood!"

There was strength and courage and conviction in the challenge. The tense men who heard it first nodded in sober agreement, then burst into cheers and applause.

Still holding to her father's arm, Anne watched eagerly as the men came out of the capitol building. How could she know which man was Governor Mason? She must see him!

Even if no one had pointed him out, she was sure she would have recognized him. But the crowd about her all were eager to shake his hand or wave to him in greeting. His blue-gray eyes moved quickly from face to face, lighting as he spoke to those he knew. His waving, dark brown hair was worn long and combed back from a high, broad forehead. There was a hint of a dimple in his chin and his lips, so firmly set now, were surely meant for laughter. A close-fitting black coat and trousers revealed a fine, strong frame.

"Isn't he brave, Papa?" Anne whispered.

"Defiant, I'd say," her father replied.

"Papa, I don't want to go to Ohio. I want to stay in Michigan."

"Have you fallen under the spell of this young 'Hotspur Governor' already?" he asked, with the familiar arch of his eyebrows.

Suddenly the men around them seemed to be pushing them forward. In another moment Anne and her father were standing face to face with Stevens Thompson Mason.

"Two new Wolverines, Governor," the older man said, laying a hand on Papa's shoulder. "I don't know their names yet. They just came in on the steamer this morning."

Anne gasped. She and Papa were being introduced to the Governor of Michigan Territory. With no formality at all! By a man who had never seen them before and who didn't even know their names. She couldn't believe this was happening.

"I'm Martin Rogers, Governor, and this is my daughter, Anne. We're from New York State," she heard her father saying.

Governor Mason extended his hand to Papa, then bowed sedately to Anne, as he might to any lady of quality.

"Welcome to Michigan," he said, and his eyes as well as his lips were smiling. "Your occupation, sir?"

"A tradesman, Governor," Papa replied. "A peddler, they call us back where I came from."

"I'm glad to hear that," Governor Mason said. "Michigan needs tradesmen. Our trade and commerce are just opening up. And our schools are just getting organized, too. You bring a family, I see."

"Two families," Papa said. "Mine and my sister's. Schools are important to us, Governor."

"Schools are of major importance to the State," the Governor assured him. "We believe that a uniform and liberal system of common schools, open to all, is the surest basis of public happiness and prosperity. Our new constitution will make provision for the extension of the blessings of education to all classes in the community."

"Gov'ner, you sure do make it sound mighty fine," a voice in the crowd called out cheerfully. "Half the time I don't know the meanin' of what yer sayin' but I'm fer ya. All the time!"

The men laughed, and Governor Mason's seriousness gave way to friendly laughter too.

"Mr. Rogers, won't you join some of your new neighbors at the Mansion House tonight?" Governor Mason suggested. "Or perchance you'll find a livelier crowd at the Steamboat Hotel. You're sure to find friendly companionship wherever men gather, here in Michigan."

Then a new group of men pushed forward to claim his attention, and he lifted his hat in a dignified salute to Papa and Anne.

Anne looked up at her father. He took a handkerchief from his pocket and carefully wiped his forehead.

"Did you ever meet a Governor before, Papa?" Anne whispered as they walked slowly back toward the city.

"No, I never did, Anne," Papa admitted. "This one's a powerful spell-binder, for a certainty. But there's more I'd like to know about him and his Michigan, and this Ohio business, too."

"I think he'd have talked to you more, if those others hadn't crowded in," Anne said. "I think he liked you."

"He has a convincing way of making you think he likes you," Papa replied. "Maybe that's one trait politicians and peddlers have in common."

"No, I think he liked you," Anne said. "And I think he's right and the clown is wrong about Michigan. I want to join forces with Governor Mason."

"Are you going to be the kind who must have a 'cause'?" Papa asked. His laugh was hearty and reassuring, and he gave her shoulder a gentle shove. "You run along back to the boat. I'll see what I can find out at this Mansion House your fine-sounding Governor talked about."

Anne did not run. She walked very slowly, thinking hard about what she had heard that afternoon. Trying to remember every word. Papa would have to decide right away whether to go on to Ohio or cast his lot with Stevens Thompson Mason and Michigan. They couldn't stay on the boat more than one night, for it was starting back to Buffalo as soon as the Captain could re-load.

"Oh, let it be Michigan," Anne prayed silently. "Dear Lord, let it be Michigan!"

CHAPTER

2

Chicago Turnpike

Anne rode with her sandy-haired, freckled cousin Nate in the heavy Conestoga wagon, now loaded with Polly's household goods, as Martin Rogers led his party out of Detroit. He still had doubts about Michigan's Boy Governor. Anne had heard him say so honestly to Uncle Luther. But Ohio was old and settled up. Michigan was new and soon to be a state — a state of promise. So now they were headed westward along the Chicago Turnpike.

Once Anne would have sat proudly beside her father on the seat of his peddler's wagon, singing with him as they rode along. Now Polly sat there, and by right, Anne knew. It hadn't been necessary for anyone to tell Anne where she should ride. She had gone to the second wagon without bidding when the teams lined up on the road that led from the dock to the Turnpike. But she did it with a hurt inside that she would not have admitted to anyone.

Behind Anne and Nate came Uncle Luther and Aunt

Ellen with the twins, Luther and Lucy. All their house-hold goods and farm tools were crowded onto one wagon.

Anne stroked the warm, soft fur of a half-grown gray and white kitten that climbed restlessly from her shoulder to her lap as they bumped along the rough corduroy road.

"That cat should be back on the load keeping mice and rats away from Polly's stuff," Nate said, disapprovingly. Nate was sixteen now, the oldest of the cousins, and lately he seemed to feel he should express disapproval of everything the others did.

"Mittens has been guarding her stuff ever since we left New York State," Anne answered. "He has a right to ride up front now, if he wants to. Isn't he pretty, Nate? See how even the markings are on his face and down his neck and on his little hands."

"Paws," Nate corrected. "He's pretty enough, I guess. What I'm wondering is what're you going to do with all this stuff of Polly's now that you've got it here."

Anne looked at the houses on either side of the road. They were at the edge of Detroit now, and ahead stretched miles of farming land, much of it still to be cleared of trees. Bark-covered log houses were all she saw, the corners of the logs sawed off close and neat. They were picturesque enough, but very small and no one of them would house all of Polly's household goods.

"I never did understand why Polly set such store by this furniture," Anne admitted. "She guards it as though there was something special about it."

"Don't you know?" Nate asked, his gray-green eyes peering at her from under the broad brim of his hat.

"Know what?"

"Polly had to go to court to get it, after her folks died," Nate told her. "Her brother Eb was going to put her out of the family with nothing at all."

"Why?" Anne asked in surprise.

"Don't you know?" he asked again.

"Of course not. I wouldn't ask if I knew," Anne answered impatiently. "Why, Nate?"

Nathan Crawford hesitated, his thin features contracted in thought.

"Why, Nate?" Anne pressed.

"Because she ran away and married your Paw, that's why," he replied at last.

Anne felt as though a tight hand had clamped suddenly about her throat. She couldn't believe she had heard aright. And she couldn't answer Nate at all.

"Are you mad at me because I told you?" he asked at last, and his voice was a little husky and unnatural.

Anne hugged the kitten tighter in her arms. She had known there was something different about Polly's brother Eb. But not that he hated her father so much.

"I'm not mad at you," she said at last. "Granny said Polly came from an awfully good family. I knew there was something."

"I guess they had a lot of money once," Nate said in explanation. "Still have, maybe. I heard Paw say they had a shipping business in Boston. Associated with governors and such folks. Her brother Eb's a lawyer, too."

"How did Polly get the furniture away from him, then?" Anne asked. "Did she get another lawyer?"

Nate hesitated. "I wasn't there, Anne," he finally said.

"But you know."

Nate's forehead wrinkled in thought again.

"If I know, maybe you've a right to know too," he said at last. "Your Paw got a lawyer for her and went to court with her. My Paw says Uncle Mart ought-a been a lawyer. Paw says it was Uncle Mart that got the court to allow her everything in the old mansion where they lived. Uncle Mart did more than the lawyer, Paw says."

Anne stared at the wild countryside in silence. Blue iris nodded in the wind. Green sumach grew nearly as tall as the sapling walnut and hickory and maple trees on either side of the wide clearing that had been cut when the road was built to connect the forts at Detroit and Chicago. Anne had heard the Captain on the boat telling Papa about the road. Ten years ago it was built, when Lewis Cass was governor of the Territory and there was fear of Indian uprisings like the Black Hawk War. Odd that the story should come back to her mind now as she rode along behind Papa and Polly.

Polly must really love him, to have defied her brother Eb and left a mansion in Boston, Anne realized. She might have to live in a log house now. Perhaps Polly loved him as much as she, Anne, did. But how could she? Papa was Anne's own. He had always been, ever since she could remember. How could Polly love him as she did?

And Eb! He didn't think Papa was good enough for Polly. That was it!

Anne couldn't let Nate see the tell-tale crimson that flushed her cheeks and throat when the awful sense of humiliation came to her. Papa having to defend himself against Heaven knew what, because he had married Polly. Anne lifted the kitten from her lap to her shoulder and hid her hot cheek against his soft, comforting side.

"Anne! Look! To the right."

Nate jarred her back to immediate realities. "Don't be frightened. Just look," he said.

Standing beside the road and staring at them silently were half a dozen Indians. All wore blankets around their shoulders, held down at the waist by leather or woolen belts. Their moccasins were decorated with colored quills and red or blue cloth leggings encased their legs from ankles to above the knees, leaving their thighs bare. Tobacco pouches and scalping knives hung from the braves' belts. There was only one squaw in the group. A shapeless, gray calico dress sagged unevenly below her blanket and she carried a papoose on her back.

The Indians did not make any move toward the travelers, but stared unemotionally as the wagons rolled past.

"What do you suppose they're thinking?" Nate asked in a low voice.

Anne shook her head.

"Papa says this road follows the paths their forefathers beat through the forest years ago," she told him. "The Indians used to go once a year to the British forts for gifts. Thousands of Indians, I guess."

"Why should the British give them gifts?" Nate asked. "Why would anyone give them gifts?"

"So they wouldn't take sides with the French against the British, of course," Anne said. "You know that. And to prevent massacres."

Nate nodded. "I'd forgotten."

"That was before Michigan was a Territory even, I guess," Anne went on. "Now Governor Mason's going to make us a state."

At the thought of Governor Mason, Anne brightened. "Aren't you glad Papa decided to continue on into Michigan as he'd planned?" she asked, and for the first time on the trip she smiled cheerfully.

Nate shrugged his thin shoulders.

"Paw was glad," he said. "He wants to get a good farm cheap. He says he can get farming land at the government land office at White Pigeon. They opened it up four years ago, and land's selling for two dollars an acre there. Fifty cents an acre is all he'll have to pay down. Or he can go on to the land office at Kalamazoo. They opened that one up last year."

"And Papa can get his business started early, ahead of everyone else," Anne said.

"But what are we going to do out here, Anne?" Nate asked. "You and me. What are we going to do?"

"We can help Governor Mason make Michigan a great state," Anne answered somewhat uncertainly.

"How? Tell me how?" Nate pressed.

How indeed?

Beyond the clearing that flanked each side of the Turnpike lay a rough, tree-covered wilderness for the most part. Pieces of broken wagons and ruined axe-handles littered the roadside, abandoned where the accidents had happened. And the road did fall out from under them as the clown had said. More than once Anne had thought the straining teams would not be able to pull the heavy wagon out of the rut into which the wheels had sunk. There were places where the logs, which were the foundation of this military road, were completely buried under a foot or more of mud.

Anne watched the rhythmic motion of the horses' broad bay rumps and the ceaseless swish of their long, dark tails. The familiar acrid odor of those sweating bodies was reassuring. Horses and wagons, towns and farms and good roads like those they had back in New York State — that was what Stevens Thompson Mason wanted for Michigan. But when she tried to put it into words, Nate found her explanations unconvincing.

"But you and me, Anne? What are we going to do?" he repeated.

Anne didn't know.

"I never said this to Paw, but I don't want to farm!" Nate told her in sudden, unexpected confidence. "I never wanted to come to Michigan at all. If we've got to live here, I wish we could-of stayed in Detroit."

Anne looked at him in surprise. Everybody expected Nate to be a farmer and to help Uncle Luther with the long hours of hard work on the new farm in Michigan. But now, as Anne looked at the thin legs braced against the buckboard, and the long, slender hands that held the reins, she realized that Nate was not built to pull stumps and haul rocks and hold a plough to a furrow.

"What do you want to do, Nate?" she asked.

"I don't know. But in Detroit I could have found something. You know what? Polly got a 'Detroit Gazette' yesterday while you and Uncle Mart were at the circus. She said there were museums and public gardens and churches and schools in Detroit. She read about them."

"She did?" Anne asked in surprise.

"And lyceums and literary societies and theaters. I think Polly'd like to have stayed in Detroit. She read about how it's growing and how they need mechanics."

"Would you like to be a mechanic?" Anne asked.

"I don't know. All I know is that I don't want to farm!"

Nate's voice was husky with emotion and he held the reins in a fierce grip as though he half-feared, half-hated the horses.

Suddenly Anne felt very close to him. He knew what a dreadful thing had happened in her family and he had a terrible problem too.

"Nate, what are we going to do?" she asked in near-panic. "I can't stay at home all alone with Polly when Papa's away on his long trips. You know how much he's away. What are we going to do, Nate?"

CHAPTER

3

Country School

Papa stopped at every crossroads, wherever he saw a store and a grist mill. Ten Eyck's Tavern, then Ypsilanti, then Wallace's Tavern where they spent the first night. Everywhere he asked the same questions. How was business? Where did the merchants get their goods? How did they haul them? And because he was so friendly and his manner so easy, men were willing to stop their work and talk to him.

Usually Anne left Nate's wagon at these stops to stand beside Papa, while Polly bent forward from her place at the driver's seat to listen and observe, with an eye which Anne soon learned missed no details.

"You'll find a city map on every tavern wall from here to Chicago," the innkeeper at Ypsilanti told him. "Courthouses and warehouses, and even piers and steamers drawn in, if the place is on a river. But all you'll actually find is a few log huts, some of 'em shingled, mebbee, and wolves, and Indians with feathers in their braids."

"Not many stores, then?" Papa persisted.

"Oh, yes, you'll find a few stores. Codfish an' whiskey an' tobacco is their stock. They get it in Detroit an' they haul it out theirselves."

Papa looked appraisingly at Ypsilanti's main street, that ran close to the river. "Promising town you have here," he said.

"We're quite a place now," the innkeeper agreed. "But this used to be a hard town back in the early days. Woodruff's Grove 'twas called, an' the settlers poled their way up the Huron River back in 1823 to git here. Brung what little goods they had with 'em. No church nor school like we've got now. Couple of corn mills was about all they had. Pitchin' quoits along the river bank an' drinkin' was the life. You foller the river on about a mile an' a ferry'll take you acrost. Sorry I ain't got no room for you."

The Great Western stage coach, that started daily from Detroit for Chicago, had already passed them. Hauled by four horses, it made the full trip in five days, barring bad weather. Other emigrant wagons had gone ahead too, while Papa stopped to talk. Anne wondered if there would be room for them at Wallace's Tavern, where the innkeeper had directed them.

The two sleeping rooms, one for men and one for women and children, still had empty beds when they arrived, but no breakfast was promised so they agreed to start early the next morning and breakfast in Tecumseh as others planned to do. Anne was starving when they arrived and the breakfast of wild strawberries, coffee and corn bread was good.

"You might make Jonesville by night," the Tecumseh innkeeper told Papa. "Benaiah Jones has the biggest tavern in the country. Started his place back in 1828 at a point where the Turnpike crosses the St. Joe river."

"Jonesville's quite a town now, I heard back down the road," Papa said. "They've got a school and church as well as stores, I'm told. And a grist mill and saw mill and tannery. Is that right?"

The innkeeper nodded. "First real stock of goods in this part of the country opened for sale there last year," he said. "They ain't really got a church yet, though. Both the Methodists and Presbyterians hold meetings in the school house, but I hear the Presbyterians is fixin' to build this year."

Polly nodded approvingly at this news.

"If you don't make Jonesville by night, Capt. Moses Allen'll likely take you in," the innkeeper continued. "You'll come to his place first. There wasn't a white man between Allen's Prairie and the North Pole when he settled here in '26. Old soldier, he be. War of 1812. White Pigeon's about fifty miles beyond his place."

Nate had left the table while Papa was questioning the talkative innkeeper. When they went to the wagons he was nowhere in sight. Papa and Uncle Luther both called his name but there was no answer.

Anne walked back toward the edge of town, looking down the road they had just traversed. He couldn't have run away! Could he possibly have started back to Detroit?

She stopped as the road made a turn around a clump of trees. He was not to be seen. From behind came the sound of hurrying steps crunching the gravel, and Anne turned to see Polly hastening toward her.

"Did he say anything to cause you to think he'd run away?" Polly asked directly, and the suddenness of the question caught Anne off guard. But she couldn't betray Nate.

"No. Why no. What would make you think that?" Anne asked.

"He was talking to you — well, earnestly," Polly said and she seemed to be peering into Anne's very mind.

"He never mentioned running away," Anne said with conviction, recalling that this was indeed true. "I — I just don't know where to look."

"I've a feeling Nate's heart isn't in this venture," Polly persisted.

From the edge of town came the sound of Uncle Luther calling Nate's name, and just then the boy emerged from one of the little log houses. Anne pointed toward him with relief. He stood in the doorway talking until Anne and Polly reached him, and when he turned to them his gray-green eyes were shining.

"I've been talking with Cousin Jake," he explained. "I saw a sign over his door when we came into town. It said 'Cousin Jake. Chairs for Sale. Come In.' So I went back to see him."

"What did you see?" Anne asked.

"Just what the sign said," Nate replied. "Chairs. Every other house in Tecumseh is a chair factory, Cousin Jake said. Most of the emigrants don't bring enough furniture, and what they do bring gets broke. Cousin Jake said they sell all they can make."

"We don't need chairs, for a certainty," Polly observed.

"You don't. But Maw hasn't too many and I could make her some if I had one or two tools."

"Papa can get tools if you want them," Anne assured him as she climbed onto the wagon and with Nate started the drive out of town. "Likely he has what you need already."

They reached Jonesville that night. Benaiah Jones and his agreeable wife welcomed all comers. Their tavern yard was crowded with wagons, and had the appearance of an emigrant camp when Papa brought his party to a halt there. Anne could see, in the twilight, heavy white-topped wagons with oxen grazing beside them, and lighter vehicles like Papa's, with sleek and well-groomed horses. Mr. Jones looked the Rogers outfit over appraisingly. Apparently he judged the circumstances of the travelers by their wagons and animals, and the quantity of goods they brought with them. But he treated them all alike, and as in all the inns along the Turnpike, the men slept in one big room downstairs, the women and children on the second floor. It was from Benaiah Jones that Papa learned of a good location.

"Go on down the Turnpike a spell," Jones told him. "You'll come to an oak opening where there's a settlement getting started. Half a dozen families are there already, and they've got a school where you can send all these younguns. It might even be a town some day. It's on the way to White Pigeon and the land office you inquired about. The best land's been bought up already, but there's some up for re-sale."

Papa suggested leaving the women and children at Jonesville while he explored the site, but Anne begged to go with him.

"I haven't had a chance to ride with you since we left New York State," she said, trying not to make too much of a point of it.

Papa gave her one of his searching looks.

"That's right, you haven't," he agreed. "It makes me feel good that you remembered. Climb up on the old wagon and off we'll go to Jerico!" And he raised his hand in the familiar gesture that she loved.

Anne's heart sang again. Polly was forgotten, and Nate, and all the worries that had beset her. The sky was bright and the thrushes sang in the trees beside the winding road that cut the forest land ahead. Red deer darted out of their way and black wolverines, at once shy and mischievous, watched at the edges of the clearing.

Papa sang buoyantly and his strong baritone rang clear and echoed through the trees.

> "Green grow the rushes, O!
> Kiss her quick and let her go."

And he bent over Anne to give her a quick kiss on the cheek.

"Oh, Papa, I love you so!" Anne burst out, and then unexpectedly all the pent-up emotion of days and weeks came pouring out in hysterical words and smiles and tears. "I love you, and I'm so proud of you!"

She put her arm as far around his broad back as it would go. Just the feel of his worsted coat was reassuring.

"And I love you, Anne. I've been proud of the way you've carried yourself, these past weeks," he said, suddenly quiet. "Very proud. You're going to make a fine woman."

Anne swallowed hard. She must always conduct herself so Papa would be proud. She wouldn't cry. Why should she, when she was so happy?

But there was no time to think more about it. A bend in the road and there, in a grassy opening, a newly-built school house was set down. It was the first one they had seen along the Turnpike.

Papa stopped his team.

"Anne, why don't you go in and look the school over, while I drive on to the settlement. It's bound to be around the next bend."

"This road does twist and turn, doesn't it?" Anne asked, looking at the school house questioningly, and a little reluctant to leave her father.

"The surveyors followed the Indian trails," Papa explained. "The Indians knew where to ford the rivers and how to get between the lakes. Seems to me the word 'Michigan' means 'many lakes' or 'great water' or something like that in the Chippewa language. Anyway, you look at the school while I survey the situation at the settlement. I'll be back in a couple of hours."

Anne jumped down from the wagon and with a wave to her father, walked toward the school house. No one noticed her at first as she stood in the doorway. When the nearest children saw her, there was a whispering and flutter of excitement that spread from bench to bench until the harassed young girl who was hearing a recitation at last took note of it. She did not seem to welcome the intrusion. C348240 CO. SCHOOLS

"May I come in?" Anne asked. "We're planning to settle near here. Likely I'll be coming to school soon, and my cousins too."

"Take a seat then, do," the teacher said, trying to be polite. "Now class, proceed."

The desks had been made by driving pins into the walls and placing planks on them, one leg supporting the outer edge of the plank. Seats were fashioned in the same manner and the whole room had the clean odor of resin and fresh lumber. A shallow box of sand served as a blackboard. Two small windows and the open door let in shafts of sunlight. The restless youngsters wriggled and turned to look at Anne, instead of paying heed to their lessons. The teacher's patience clearly was already worn ragged. She was young, not much older than Anne she appeared, with delicate features and black hair that waved, lace-like, around the white oval of her face.

Sitting near the door, Anne suddenly was aware of a little girl standing uncertainly at the entrance.

"Teacher," she whispered, but her voice did not carry beyond the first row of desks. "Teacher," she repeated but no one listened to her, and she turned and went out of the school building.

Anne had an uneasy feeling that something was wrong. Quietly she slipped from the bench where she had been sitting and followed the child into the school yard.

"What's the matter?" Anne asked.

"Baby's in the well," the little girl replied.

"What?" Anne reached for the child's arm and looked at her in alarm. "What?" she repeated.

"In the well," and the child pointed toward a pile of dirt at the back of the school building that indicated recent excavation. Anne had not observed it when she came into the school yard.

Running to the open well, Anne peered in. At first she saw nothing, but bending over and shielding her eyes from the sun, she was sure she saw a bit of cloth floating on top of the water.

How deep was the water in this well? Anne looked about for a pole, or some other device she could use to gauge the depth of the water. There was none, nor any safe means by which she could lower herself into the well. She wondered about the equipment in the school house, and thought of the nervous teacher. What help would she be?

"Daddy's over there," the child beside her said, as though reading her thoughts. "He's cutting down trees."

Anne's eyes followed the extended hand. She could, indeed, hear the ring of axe blows, not too far distant.

"Wait here and be quiet," Anne said. "And don't go near the well." Then, running as fast as she could, she set off through the trees toward the reassuring sounds. This was best, she thought, as she scrambled through the brush. The distressed teacher would not have been able to help.

"Come!" Anne called as she drew near the place where crash of steel against timber promised help. "Come quick!"

The axe sounds stopped.

"Come to the school house," Anne called breathlessly.

The brush parted, and a large, dark-haired man stared at her in astonishment.

"Oh, hurry," Anne begged. "I think there's a child in the well. One of the little girls told me there's a child in the well."

Without speaking the man rushed ahead of her. He was already in the well when Anne reached the school yard. By the side of the embankment the little girl still stood, staring in fear yet not quite comprehending the tragedy.

Anne turned the child's back to the well, and moved her away gently. She held the trembling little body against her own firm legs, and struggled to control her frightened breathing.

It was only a matter of seconds and the man was out of the well and standing beside her, water dripping from his hips and legs.

"She's dead." His voice was thick and scarcely audible. "She's my neighbor's only child. Who are you?"

"I'm Anne Rogers. I came to school for the first time this afternoon. My father's at the settlement."

"You go inside and tell the teacher. Tell her to bring Amanda home," and he indicated the little girl who was clinging to Anne's skirts. "I'll take the other one, Lord bless us and save us." Then putting his large hand gently on the child's head he added, "Amanda, you do as I say, now. The teacher'll bring you home."

Anne did not speak for a few moments. She held Amanda's shoulders in her own strong hands until she was sure the man and his sad burden were gone. Odd that the child had not tried to go with her father, Anne thought, but as she looked into the frightened little face she thought perhaps she understood. Amanda sensed that something was terribly wrong.

"What's your name?" Anne asked her. "Your full name?"

"Amanda. Amanda Doyle."

"Come, Amanda."

Anne walked slowly across the yard to the school house. Strange that the robins still sang, that the blue lupines still nodded in the sun. She would have to call the teacher outside to tell her what had happened. It would be wrong to alarm all of the children.

Anne cleared her throat as she stood in the doorway, but the teacher did not look up.

"Teacher," Anne said clearly at last. "Mr. Doyle has just been here. He asked me to give you a message. Please come outside."

The teacher put aside her book and looked at Anne, a worried expression on her face.

"Please come outside," Anne repeated and there was an urgency in her voice that brought the teacher to the door.

"What's the meaning of this?" she questioned, looking from Anne to Amanda.

Quietly Anne told her what had happened.

"Mr. Doyle said for you to bring Amanda home," she said when she had finished the tragic story.

The teacher's face grew white with horror. Her lips framed the one word, "drowned," but the barest sound came forth. Suddenly she raised both hands to her head and with a frightened cry ran from the school yard and down the Turnpike, leaving Anne and Amanda and the school house behind her.

Anne stood near the door, holding Amanda's cold little hand, uncertain for a moment what to do. Through the doorway she could see the children twisting in their seats and craning their necks to see what was happening outside. What was she to tell them? Then she thought of Papa. In another hour he would be there, and he would know what to do. Certainly she could manage for one hour.

Still holding Amanda by the hand she walked into the room, and to the teacher's bench. She lifted the child to a seat near her and picked up the book the teacher had put aside. It was an arithmetic book, and Anne knew about where the lesson had left off.

"We'll just go on with the recitations now," she said in as firm a voice as she could command. "Teacher had to go to the settlement. It was important business."

She was a stranger to them, so the youngsters quieted, waiting to see what manner of person she was. And in that moment Anne felt a surge of confidence. Going to the sand box she drew a ladder for them, then called the arithmetic class to her side. This was the way Papa had taught her to add. She could teach them the same way.

"You're on the first rung of this ladder now. If you climb up two more rungs, where will you be?"

It was easy that way. They could add one and two, and two and four. She would teach arithmetic until Papa came. She glanced ahead in the book to see what the next class might be doing. All she had to do was keep ahead of them. And they were interested, eager to see what she was going to do next.

A shadow in the doorway drew Anne's attention from her sand box. She looked up to see Mr. Doyle standing there. The teacher hadn't taken Amanda home, so he had come back for her, of course. She led the child down the aisle, between the rough benches, to him. Then she looked at Mr. Doyle for the first time. She had been too frightened really to see him before.

He was a young man, tall and broad-shouldered, and with a heavy beard on his chin and along his cheeks. He wiped the perspiration from his forehead with the back of a rough, calloused hand, then wiped his hands on his trousers. Blue eyes he had, and a long thin nose. Papa would say the map of Ireland was on his face.

"I came for Amanda, yes," he said, "but I was observin' of you now. And did you say your folks has come to the settlement?"

"Yes, that's where my father is now."

"And would he be fixin' to locate here?"

"Unless he's changed his mind just this afternoon," Anne told him.

"The teacher's left," Mr. Doyle said after a pause. "She boarded 'round, of course, and she was at our place this week. She's packed her satchel and is waiting for the stage coach. I'm the school moderator, and I was wondering if she'd made up the rate bills. Tuition's due on Friday nights."

"I don't know, but I can look," Anne said: "If she has, I can find them."

Anne went back to the front of the room and looked through the papers on the teacher's desk. There were few enough of them, and scarce a half-dozen books in the school, all told. The rate bills were there, one for each family with children in the school, so she took them to Mr. Doyle.

"Might I ask, have you ever taught school?" he inquired as she handed the papers to him.

Anne shook her head.

"As I understand the law, every schoolmaster is to furnish instruction in French and reading and writing and arithmetic, and good manners. You was furnishing good instruction in arithmetic all right. And could you do the rest now?" He looked at her critically. "You've got good manners, 'tis easy to see."

Anne was not altogether certain what he meant, but she said "yes."

"We was prepared to pay $14 a month and board the teacher, but if your folks should be living here, you'd board at home. I don't exactly know what the school board would agree to pay, with no board to give. But I'm of a mind you'd be a better teacher than the last one. Would you be liking the job?"

The blood began to pound in Anne's temples and there was a queer feeling in her stomach. Mr. Doyle was asking her to teach the school! Of course she would like the job.

"Yes, sir," she said.

"And where are your folks staying? At Jones' Tavern?"

"Yes, sir," Anne answered again.

"And you said your name is Rogers? Anne Rogers?"

Anne nodded.

"I'll talk to the board then, and I'll be a-seeing you. I'll take Amanda home now. You can dismiss the school if you like."

"How long was school supposed to last?" Anne asked.

" 'Till four o'clock. But you can let it out any time."

"I'll keep school until four o'clock then," Anne replied. "Good day, Mr. Doyle. And . . . I'm awfully sorry for everyone."

House Raisin'

The first time Anne ever heard **Polly** really speak her mind was when Papa told her about the school at the settlement. It was several days after Mr. Doyle had asked her to teach the school and she had not heard anything more from him. Papa, in the meantime, had been busy day and night with arrangements for a house-raising at the site he had selected on the Turnpike.

It was evening, and Polly and Papa were sitting under one of the big trees in the tavern yard at Jonesville when Anne, her kitten on her shoulder, joined them.

"Have you heard anything more from Mr. Doyle?" Papa asked her unexpectedly, and without waiting for more than a shake of her head, he turned to Polly.

"The school moderator at the settlement has asked Anne to teach the school," he explained to her. "I guess I forgot to tell you, in the rush of trying to get a house up and all the other plans."

Polly dropped her knitting into her lap, her eyes round with surprise.

"But she's only a child, Mr. Rogers," she protested. "Anne hasn't finished school herself yet. She's not prepared to teach. It had been in my mind, if all went as we plan, that she might go back to Troy to Miss Emma Willard's School for Girls. Next year, perhaps."

That Polly had been thinking about her, and making plans for her, was almost as great a surprise to Anne as Mr. Doyle's offer had been. But it was not welcomed. Without reason Anne felt resentment. She looked quickly from Polly to her father. He was looking at Polly almost in amazement.

Papa had listened quietly when Anne told him about the drowning and Mr. Doyle's offer, while they rode back to Jones' Tavern after it all had happened. Now and then he had nodded his head and once or twice he had asked a question.

"When the big boys start school in the winter, after the farm work's done, will you mind that?" he asked. "Some of them will be bigger than you, and older too, likely as not. Right mischievous too, and hard to handle."

Anne hadn't thought about the big boys. Only little children had been in school that day, and winter seemed far off. Still, the idea of the big boys didn't frighten her.

Then he had asked her about the school laws and whether she had talked to Mr. Doyle about them.

"I don't rightly know much about the school laws in Michigan," he said. "Some time back, in Governor Cass' administration, there was a national land grant for schools in the Territory. The legislation provided that every township with fifty families should be provided with a good schoolmaster. It seems to me the teacher was to give instruction in French as well as reading and writing and arithmetic. But I'm not sure."

"Why should the children learn French?" Anne asked. "I can't see any sense to that." Anne knew no French.

"The French were the earliest settlers in Detroit, and that old law was passed when about all the white people in the Territory lived around Detroit. Maybe they don't hold to it out here. What I was really wondering about is your age. Did Mr. Doyle say whether the law had any provision about age?"

"He didn't say much about the law," Anne admitted. "He didn't say anything about my age."

"Well, I'm glad you're thinking about it seriously," Papa had said, and Anne knew right well he wasn't satisfied that she should do it. He hadn't mentioned it to her again until this evening.

"When I was at the settlement today, I heard they were holding a meeting about getting a new teacher. I don't know what they decided, but it set me to wondering. Are you still of a mind to do it, Anne? In case the others agreed with Mr. Doyle?"

"Yes," Anne told him without any hesitation. "I haven't changed my mind."

Papa rubbed his hands together thoughtfully, and Polly picked up her knitting.

"That idea about the girls' school back in Troy," Papa said at last. "Now I hadn't thought of that. But it's a fine school, I know. What do you think about that, Anne?"

"I hadn't thought about it at all," Anne said. "But anyway, that would be next year or the year after. Meantime I can be helping with all the plans for developing Michigan. We heard Governor Mason talk about them in Detroit. I'll be just like you and Uncle Luther and the other people."

Anne sensed disapproval in the silence that followed.

"Governor Mason said schools are of major importance to a state," Anne said, bolstering her arguments with the important-sounding words she remembered so well. "He said a lot about schools. He believes everyone in the Territory should go to school."

"Anne, that's all true," her father said at last. "And I'm proud that you want to do something for the state where we've come to live. Something worth while. We should all want to do more than just earn a living. When I carry my goods from home to home along the Turnpike, I like to feel that I'm bringing the best the East has manufactured out here to this new country. So if you want to help your Governor Mason with all the noble plans we heard about, I'm not against it. Teaching would be a fine way to do it, and no mistake. But Anne, not until you're prepared for it."

Anne knew, then, that the decision had been made. Papa had agreed with Polly. But she couldn't quite admit it.

"Mr. Doyle thinks I'm prepared," she told him. "He said I'd be a better teacher than the one they had."

"But he didn't know you were just turned fifteen.

You're big for your age, Anne. He didn't know you'd never gone beyond the common school back home," Papa reminded her.

"You taught me most of what I know. More than I ever learned in school, and you — "

"Anne!"

Almost never did Anne give Papa occasion to speak sharply to her. But her heart had been set on teaching the school. She had dreamed about it ever since the moment Mr. Doyle had asked her if she wanted the job. Never had she thought of what she might do when she grew up, until that day. Since then she had thought of nothing else.

She could see herself standing in front of the room hearing recitations — making pictures in the sand box — correcting the mistakes — helping those who were slow. Whenever she thought of Stevens Thompson Mason she recalled what he had said about schools, and the conviction in his voice when he said it. Some day he might know that she was a teacher. He'd feel that she was part of his great plan for Michigan. In one glorious day dream she had pictured him riding along the Turnpike and stopping at the school. She had seen him standing in the doorway and observing her as she helped the little boys and girls with their lessons. Papa would be proud of her then, too. He'd see that Stevens Thompson Mason was right. Papa would be on the Governor's side too.

Mittens jumped from her shoulder to roll in the grass and bat at fallen leaves. The first fireflies of evening flashed their sparks, and he leaped and scrambled after them. Miserably she followed him as he scampered across the yard.

"Anne, I think Mr. Doyle and another man are driving up now," her father called to her.

Anne couldn't face them. What was she to say? "I'm sorry, Mr. Doyle, but I'm not old enough." After the confidence with which she had told him that she would teach the school?

"You tell them, Papa. Please," Anne begged, and picking up Mittens she carried him to the shed where he must spend the night in the big wagon with Polly's household goods.

Anne went to the upstairs room of the Inn early, but Polly was already there. On the bed beside her were some long strips of white cotton cloth.

"The house-raising tomorrow will be a big day for your father," Polly said without looking at Anne. "It'll be the start of his business in Michigan."

"Yes, Ma'am," Anne said and bent down to remove her shoes and stockings.

"There'll be a lot for us to do, what with the cooking and feeding all the men."

Anne knew that was true. "I'll do my part, Polly, Ma'am," she said.

"And in the evening they always have a dance on the new floor, Mrs. Jones tells me," Polly continued as she brushed her curls and pinned them down in careful rolls about her head. "A floor dance, they call it."

Anne hadn't heard about that. "A floor dance?" she questioned.

–48–

"Mrs. Jones says it's customary," Polly replied. "She let me have a sadiron today and I've gone over our best dresses. But it's going to be hard to look right neat and appealing after cooking over the open pit, I'm afraid."

"You always look nice," Anne said, half-heartedly.

It was difficult for Anne to adjust herself to the idea that Polly was thinking about her. Pressing her clothes. Planning for her. To go to Miss Willard's school would have been a wonderful thing to dream about if Anne hadn't set her heart on teaching the settlement school. Or if Papa had planned it instead of Polly. Polly probably expected her to be grateful and to say something about it. Thank her, perhaps. But Anne couldn't think of the right way to put it, or what to say truthfully. She hadn't ever figured on Polly planning for her. Papa had always done that and she didn't want Polly to do it. Why must Polly change everything in her life? Except for Polly, Papa might not have opposed her plan to teach, Anne tried to tell herself. But she knew that wasn't true, so she dismissed the thought.

"I've a mind your father'll want us both to look as nice as we can," Polly went on, interrupting Anne's thoughts. "I suppose it will be — well, as though we were being introduced to the community. So if you'd like, I'll put your hair up on rags tonight. If you leave it until noon you'll have pretty curls for the dance at night."

How could Anne say she didn't care how her hair looked? That she wished Polly would please to just let her alone? Especially when Polly was right. Papa would look very handsome at the floor dance, Anne thought, and proudly. He would bow low and gentlemanly to all the ladies and smile at each one in turn. It would please him right well if her hair was in curls and if she looked her best, Anne knew.

Miserably she went to the footstool and sat down beside Polly.

"I'll be obliged to you then, Polly, Ma'am," she said.

Anne tied her sunbonnet down close around her head the next morning, to hide the knobs of hair, done up on rags, that circled her head.

Aunt Ellen and Uncle Luther and the little Crawfords, Papa and Polly, and Nate and Anne all drove out of the tavern yard before sun up. Men would be coming to their house-raising as soon as they'd had breakfast, and Papa must be there before they arrived, making sure all was in readiness.

Aunt Ellen was Papa's sister and like him in many ways. She had the same sturdy build and dark hair and eyes, but she didn't have Papa's easy manner. Bossy, that's what she was, Anne thought. Now she took charge of all arrangements for feeding the men who came to the house-raising.

Pits were dug and filled with logs for roasting the venison and wild turkeys that Uncle Luther and Papa had brought in the day before. There was a whole suckling pig to be roasted, and potatoes and dried corn to be boiled in the big, black iron kettles. Lumber that soon would be flooring was laid across logs and stumps for tables and benches.

"Anne, you take the young 'uns and go gather wild strawberries," Aunt Ellen directed. "We'll need a lot, so get started. Me and Polly'll manage here, with a hand from Nate when we need it."

Back along the Turnpike and in the open clearings, wild strawberries grew in great profusion. Small they were, but very sweet, and the children ate as they picked.

They followed the spreading vines farther and farther from the settlement. Woodpeckers drilled and shrilled in the trees overhead, and bright-eyed squirrels ran along branches and down tree trunks, chattering in noisy protest at the intrusion. The sun was hot on their backs and their knees ached from bending over in the grass, and their minds were lazy.

Anne saw the little Indian boy first. A naked, brown baby he was, standing at the edge of the strawberry patch, only a few feet away. She started to smile at him, but the smile froze in sudden terror. Coiled at his feet, only inches away, was a slithery black snake.

Anne suppressed a scream. Circling the menacing reptile, she grabbed the child in her arms and backed away toward the road, calling to the children to follow her.

"What's the matter, Anne?" They cried in alarm. "What's the matter?"

Anne looked for stones that she might hurl at the snake, but as she did so an arrow whirred through the branches at the edge of the clearing. The long, black whip-like body rose in the air, then lay twisting in death in the grass.

A stooped Indian, of heavy build and no longer young, came out of the woods and walked toward them.

"How, How!" he said. "Me Baw Beese."

Anne set the Indian baby down on the ground beside her, looking carefully to right and left, fearful lest another snake meet her sight.

"Me white man's friend. You Indian's friend," Baw Beese said. "You save papoose."

Anne gave the baby boy a gentle shove, but he seemed in no hurry to leave her and go to Baw Beese.

"You come to live at settlement?" Baw Beese asked her.

"We've just come," Anne replied. "We're having a house-raising and the children were helping me gather wild strawberries for dinner."

Baw Beese looked at her and the frightened Crawford cousins, now huddled near her.

"Are you a chief?" Anne asked.

Baw Beese nodded. "Topinabee big chief. Baw Beese little chief. We Pottawattamies."

"Is this your baby?" Anne asked.

"One of Baw Beese' squaws," he said. Looking at the little Crawfords he asked, "Yours?"

"They're my cousins," Anne answered. Then, not knowing whether he would understand the word she said, "No, not mine. They should be helping me gather strawberries, only I'm half afraid now. Do you think there are more snakes around here?"

"Plenty snakes," Baw Beese said. "Me take you to honey tree. Injuns get dollar for honey tree but you save papoose. Much good honey you need for much people. Come."

Anne felt no real fear in following this big, genial

Indian, but she tried to make a note of the direction in which he led her, and the children trailing after her, into the forest.

Baw Beese loked at the pails the little ones were carrying. "Need biggest pails for honey," he said. "You fix. Me get honey."

He was deft at it. Up a tree and out of sight in the green leaves, then down again with the clustering combs filled with wild dark honey. Anne divided the berries among half of the pails to make room for this new delicacy. It would be a wonderful treat. Perhaps Aunt Ellen would find a way to bake biscuits over the coals and they could serve hot biscuits and honey to the hungry men.

Anne thanked the Indian. "This will be fine for the house-raising dinner. Do you ever come to house-raisings?"

"Sometimes we watch," Baw Beese told her. "Baw Beese white man's friend."

Anne felt good about her meeting with Baw Beese and she was glad to have the honey. There were Indians all along the Turnpike and it was well to know one who was a friendly chief, she thought. She expected everyone at the settlement would be interested in her story, but when she got there no one had time to listen to her. The excavation for the cellar had been dug, the logs placed above it for the flooring, and other logs were being hauled to the site for the walls. Aunt Ellen, face shining with perspiration and excitement, was hurrying from fire to fire, preparing to get the food onto the tables.

"Back of the wagons there's a little secluded spot for

us to dress," Polly told Anne. "I'll be there in a minute to fix your hair."

All through the meal Papa's jovial voice could be heard. He called all the men by their first names and urged them to eat. Throughout the afternoon there was laughter and good-natured joking to make hard work light, and the day was pleasant. Anne forgot Baw Beese as she washed dishes and re-set the long tables, and helped prepare food for the evening meal. But when the men gathered around the newly-dug well to wash and drink before eating, he walked into the clearing, followed by four other braves.

"How, How," he said.

"Oh, Papa, this is my friend Baw Beese," Anne explained with a little pride. "He's a Pottawattamie chief, and he gave us the wild honey. I haven't had a chance to tell you."

Papa looked at her in bewilderment and she knew he was wondering how she had made the acquaintance of the Indian. Before she could explain, Mr. Doyle joined them. He had a friendly nod for Anne, a greeting for the Indian, and then he spoke to Papa.

"Baw Beese is a good Injun," he said. "His little band lives in these woods. Sure an' they'll trade you turkeys and venison and berries for flour an' corn an' 'taters any day."

Papa offered food to the Indians, and Nate and Anne filled plates for them.

"The Pottawattamies lived on reservations once, but bit by bit they've given the land up to the government," Mr. Doyle explained. "Last reservation to go was Nattawa-

Sepe. They give it up in '33, agreeing to move west to the Mississippi to a new reservation in two years. But here they still be, and no one would lay a hand on Baw Beese to make him go. Leastways not the settlers."

"How do they live?" Papa asked.

"Hunting. A little farming. A few hides to trade, maybe. I don't know if the government is still giving them money or not. The Pottawattamie chief was to get $5,000 a year for twenty years by a treaty made in Chicago back in '21.'"

"Baw Beese told me they might watch us tonight," Anne told her father.

"They'll be around all right," Mr. Doyle said. "Wherever there's food and drink you'll find 'em."

Early in the evening the women and children of the settlement began to arrive, bringing box lunches which the men would draw for partners at the midnight meal. The little tots were put to sleep in the wagons, but all women and girls from twelve to grandmothers, took part in the dancing. Two fiddlers, a drummer and a man with a mouth organ furnished the music.

Papa and Polly led the march onto the new floor, followed by Uncle Luther and Aunt Ellen, then Nate and Anne and the guests. They marched around the room and a song was started that Anne had never heard before.

> "We're all marching to Quebec,
> The drums are loudly beating.
> The Americans have gained the day,
> The British are retreating.

"The wars are o'er and we'll turn back
To the place from whence we started;
So open the ring and choose a couple in
To relieve the broken hearted."

At the words "open the ring" they all joined hands to form a ring, someone gently pushing Papa into the center. He bowed low before Anne and extended his hand to her in a gracious gesture, thus choosing her for his partner. She was glad now that her hair hung in soft, dark curls, and that Polly had patterned a grown-up dress for her, with tight bodice and full sleeves, and cut away just a trifle at the neck.

Almost without intermission the dancing continued until midnight, when the lunch boxes were brought out. Happy, exhausted revellers sat in twos on the rough benches that had been put up around the edge of the floor. No roof was yet on this house, and the stars had danced above them as they kept step to the music.

Mr. Doyle and his wife helped Polly and Aunt Ellen serve coffee from huge, smoke-covered coffee pots to the guests, who were suddenly quiet when the music stopped.

"Rogers, from the size of this floor we've laid today, some of us figure you must have it in mind to start a Tavern here at the settlement," Mr. Doyle said as he poured coffee. "An announcement of your intentions would be in order, if you care to make one."

Papa walked to the center of the new floor and looked around at his neighbors. Certainly not a man in the room was so handsome or of such a fine figure, Anne thought proudly. She scarcely listened to his words, though, as he told them of his plans to start his peddler's trade along the Turnpike. All this she knew so well, and she was tired now and content just to look at him. But she came to her senses with a start just before he finished talking.

"I realized when I reached Detroit, where the Turnpike starts, that my plans wouldn't work out just as I'd made them," Papa said. "Not for another year or two. But I learned that all the goods the merchants have must be hauled from the big stores in Detroit to the settlements in the interior. Now I have three good teams, and furniture for a 12-room house. So while I develop my trade along the Turnpike, I can furnish a hauling service too. And while the Territory is getting settled up, my good wife and daughter will indeed operate a tavern. They'll have the help of my sister and her husband, pending the time they get a farm for themselves. 'Twill be a tavern that will do credit to the community, and I give credit to Mrs. Rogers for the idea."

Anne could not believe her ears. Operate a tavern! "My good wife and daughter!"

"Nate," Anne whispered, "did you know?"

"No," he answered under his breath. "But it's better than farming. Operating a tavern's the aristocratic thing to do out here in the wilderness. Profitable, too."

"Leave it to Polly to learn that, right away!" Anne said bitterly. "But me, Nate! Polly and me! I'll have to work at her elbow all the time. Every day."

"Maybe it won't be so bad," Nate said comfortingly.

"It's the worst thing that ever happened to me!" Anne wailed. "It isn't what I want to do at all!"

It had been Polly's idea that Anne should have a room of her own and not be obliged to sleep in the big room on the second floor reserved for the women guests. She had given Anne the bed that had been hers when she lived in Boston. Made of red mahogany wood it was, that had come from Haiti. Anne had never seen such a bed. She loved the dainty, ruffled flouncings that covered the blankets and pillows and hung from the canopy. Nate admired the way it was made, with side boards adroitly morticed and tenoned. He took note, too, of the fine carving on the four posters that supported the canopy frame.

The big room down stairs was elegant with Polly's rosewood sofas and satinwood pieces. She had chairs and tables of walnut and mahogany; chests that glistened and caught the gold in the summer sunlight. There was no such furniture anywhere along the Turnpike.

To Aunt Ellen, Polly's possessions meant washing, cleaning, polishing. Most of the work had fallen on her sturdy shoulders, for Polly suffered much with fever and ague. On the hottest days in July she had shivered with unbelievable chills and had not been able to leave her bed. When the quinine at last relieved her, she was weak and tired easily.

The one time in the day when Anne was not occupied with cooking or washing was mid-afternoon. One hour at most she might have to herself before the emigrant wagons began to arrive. Then there were tired and hungry guests who wanted warm water and meals, so she must fetch and carry.

The Crawford cousins were always waiting for that hour when she was free. Up the stairway they raced to Anne's room, climbed on her bed and buried their noses in her pillows to sniff the pungent lavender sachet smell of the bed coverings. Anne would take the Clinton Primer, which guided their reading lessons, from the little drawer on top of the high chest. On the first pages there were small letters, and double letters, then the pictures and words. By following the pictures, Luther and Lucy could read sentences.

"He is a pig." Then they giggled.

"It is a wig."

"I had a dog."

"It is a hen."

The afternoon when Mr. Doyle came to ask if a political meeting might be held at the tavern was the first time Anne had known how opposed Polly was to her hour of playing school. He had brought Amanda with him and the child went to Anne at once, hugging her around the knees in friendly recognition.

"A good day to you, Missus Rogers," he said. "Is your fine husband to home?"

"No, but if there's a message, I'm expecting him in a week or ten days at most," Polly answered.

"Well, now, some of us was a-wonderin' if you'd allow a Hustings at the tavern," Mr. Doyle began. "You've the largest place at the settlement."

Polly looked her puzzlement. "A Hustings?" she asked, and she and Anne waited for the explanation which was immediately forthcoming.

"'Tis a political school, like," Mr. Doyle explained. "Folks gets together and a few who know about such things tell the rest what's a-happenin' or likely to be a-happenin'. Questions is asked and answered, for the good of all."

Polly understood then.

"Of course you can hold a Hustings here," she answered without hesitation. "Do the women attend? I hope so."

"Well, mostly they don't," Mr. Doyle admitted. "Seems like they should, now that you mention it."

With the Hustings explained, Anne turned her attention to Amanda.

"Can Amanda stay awhile and join the other children?" she asked Mr. Doyle. "They're learning to read. The twins are at lesson four in chapter four of the primer. They're six years old. How old is Amanda?"

"She's going on six, but little enough can she read,"

Mr. Doyle replied. "I still wish your Paw had let you teach the school this summer, but I can see his reasoning well enough."

"A blessing it is to get the younguns out from under foot, even for an hour," Aunt Ellen said, wiping the perspiration from her moist brow. It was late August and very hot.

Anne and her brood were on the landing and out of sight when Polly spoke.

"It worries me all the same, Sister Ellen," she said. "Anne's building up something in her mind. Her heart's still set on teaching the school, and with no teacher here yet. . . ." Polly hesitated. "Can't you both see what she's building up to? I do wish, Mr. Doyle, that you'd get a teacher. A good teacher."

"That's one of the things we must settle for sure," Mr. Doyle admitted. "We'll have Crary here for the Hustings. He wrote the part of the constitution that has to do with schools. Him and the Reverend Pierce. We can ask questions at least, and find out how to go about getting a good teacher. There's a lot we need to know, too, about what's been a-happenin' at the Capitol."

Anne was ashamed of her eaves-dropping; mortified, too, to find that Polly had so easily sensed what was in her mind. All summer the school house had squatted in the sun, closed and lifeless, because there was no teacher. And her little class could read sentences with nine words.

Anne took the primer from its place of safe-keeping. Three inches by six inches the little book was, with a hard cardboard cover. She opened it to chapter four.

"It is a boy and he has the keys," Luther and Lucy read in unison.

"Let us go in and pull the peas.

"He has the leaf of a rose.

"The keys, the peas, the leaf of a rose."

The twins stumbled, but triumphantly read the lines.

"If your Papa'll let you come over in the afternoons I'll teach you to read too, Amanda," Anne said, showing her the little letters and the roman letters and the italic letters at the front of the book.

Anne had not sensed the real significance of a Hustings when Mr. Doyle spoke to Polly about it. Her mind had been on the school, and then on Polly's determination to oppose her dream. But Nate had been talking to Mr. Doyle.

"It's a good thing we're having the meeting here," he told Anne as he brought in the wood. "Otherwise you and I wouldn't know what was said. There's too much work at the tavern for us to get away of an evening. And people out here on the Turnpike have a right to know what's happening at the Capitol."

"Is something happening?" Anne asked.

Deliberately Nate placed the wood he had been splitting in the box beside the huge kitchen fireplace. He always piled it neatly.

"Mr. Doyle says he heard the Ohio situation is worsening," Nate told her. "Everybody stops at his blacksmith shop and he hears a lot. He's the best blacksmith along

—62—

the Turnpike. He's going to bind the runners on my new sleigh with strap iron."

Anne knew Nate was spending every free minute in the shed adjoining the barn, where Papa kept his harnesses and tools. He had been getting lumber assembled and Mr. Doyle was making nails for him. At night he stretched his long frame out on the floor and drew sketches of the sleigh. It was to be curved about the back and sides, and the lines he drew were graceful. He had figured the measurements of each board that would go into it.

"Mr. Doyle's good all right," Anne conceded. "Look at the hardware he made for this house. The iron latches and the brackets for holding lamps and all. I think he took real pride in making them fancier than most people's." Then, "What does he think is going to happen over the Ohio situation?"

"He doesn't know," Nate told her. "But he doesn't trust the Whigs. They're against Governor Mason. He says our neighbor Watling is a Whig. Do you know what Watling did?"

Anne didn't know.

"Watling bought up all the land that was any good when the White Pigeon land office opened. Now he's holding it for higher prices. That's why Paw couldn't get a farm right away when we got here. I wouldn't care, only I'm sorry for Paw."

"Papa says he'll get a farm this fall or winter," Anne said reassuringly. "Right now we couldn't get along at the tavern without you and Aunt Ellen and Uncle Luther."

Anne saw Mr. Watling and some of the other neighbors for the first time the night of the Hustings. She was glad Papa had come home and was there at Polly's side to greet the people. Many of them had not been at the tavern since the house-raising, and they looked at Polly's fine things with unconcealed surprise and admiration. The drop-leaf mahogany table which usually was stretched out to seat eighteen people or more, had been closed and moved to the far end of the room near the highboy. There it served as a podium for the speakers. Polly's sofas and chairs were arranged informally, facing the table, and the entire room had more the appearance of a very fine meeting room than the combined parlor and dining room of the Inn.

Mr. Watling accepted the handsome furnishings at the tavern without comment, and with an air that seemed to say he was accustomed to elegance. The other neighbors had gathered first in little groups outside and had to be urged to come in. Mr. Watling went directly to the doorway and kept in conversation with Papa and Polly until Mr. Doyle arrived with the guest who was to speak.

"Reverend Pierce, upon my word," Mr. Watling said and proceeded to introduce the minister quite as though Mr. Doyle had not been there at all. In the background Anne and Nate watched, and they did not like Mr. Watling.

Mr. Doyle had no intention of being ignored. There was little formality about the gathering, but he had arranged it and he took charge.

"Sure and we had expected to have Isaac Crary here for

the Hustings," he announced. "As many know, it was Crary who helped write the constitution for the state and was chairman of the committee that wrote the section about the schools. He wasn't in Marshall when I got there, though, and so Reverend Pierce agreed to come in his stead. Most of you know Reverend Pierce."

There was a general nodding of heads.

"For the benefit of them that don't," Mr. Doyle went on, "he come to Marshall to be a Congregational missionary. He's been postmaster of Marshall, and he and Crary thought out the provisions that should be in the constitution to provide for schools. So he's as well qualified to talk as Crary." ·

"This whole constitution is illegal," Mr. Watling commented.

"How so?" half a dozen voices demanded.

"We had no right to hold a Constitutional Convention nor to write a state constitution at all, until the United States Congress invited us to become a state," Mr. Watling replied. "We insulted the Congress by that audacity."

"An' if we wait fer 'em to invite us, we'll be a Territory until you an' me both be dead," came a heated reply from the back of the room. "You know the Ohio bloc has been joined by the Indiany bloc and the Illinoy bloc in Congress. They ain't ever goin' to let Michigan be a state if they can help it."

"There's a Whig majority in Congress," Mr. Watling replied. "Mason's Democrats are foolhardy to oppose a strong state like Ohio and a strong majority in Congress. It will be hard enough to get approval for a free state —

and we are all agreed that Michigan is a free state — without incensing everyone in the Federal government by our illegal and unprecedented gall."

There were plenty of challenges to Mr. Watling's views.

"Ohio is trying to take Port Lawrence away from us," one man shouted. "Calling our port city 'Toledo'. Just last month Old General Stinckney's son Two Stinckney stabbed a Michigan deputy when we drove an Ohio surveying party back across the line. You think we should sit by and let that go?"

"We didn't!" another voice chimed in. "Our posse trussed up General Stinckney and his Number Two son and sent 'em back to Ohio a-hurryin'!"

There were roars of laughter as the incident was recalled.

Anne looked at Nate inquiringly. "How did all this trouble with Ohio start, Nate?" she asked. "Do you know?"

"No, but I've a mind to ask."

"You speak up then," Anne urged. "It's right for you to do it. Ask Mr. Doyle."

So Nate posed the question. How had the controversy with Ohio started?

"It's a long story," Mr. Doyle said. "Mebbee Reverend Pierce should tell it."

All eyes turned to the guest from Marshall. A big, rawboned man he was with a shining bald head and a heavy black beard that fell well down below a determined chin. He towered above everyone in the room when he rose, and there was great seriousness about him, and authority in his calm voice.

Anne learned that when Michigan was organized as a Territory in 1805 the boundary line had been fixed to run due east from the southern bend of Lake Michigan to a point on Lake Erie below Toledo. But Ohio and Indiana and Illinois all had claimed part of that territory and had included it in their boundaries when they became states. They had been settled twenty or more years ahead of Michigan. They had populated the area and Michigan had not. Ohio money had built the roads leading to Toledo and had developed the port city. Without doubt Governor Cass should have protested the first land grab, but his hands had been full with Indian forays. All of Michigan was an undeveloped wilderness except the area around Detroit, in those days. A few miles more or less along the southern border had not seemed important then. Now Michigan was developing. It was ready for statehood. Michigan did not want to give up the rich Maumee Bay area because a bigger boy was calling it his.

"This Hustings was intended to inform us about our new constitution," Mr. Doyle said, bringing the meeting back to its original purpose. "When do we vote on it?"

"October fifth and sixth. We'll ratify the constitution and elect state officers at the same time."

"Governor Mason's strategy, I hear, is to take the Toledo controversy to the United States Supreme Court as soon as we're a state," Mr. Doyle explained with pride. "Sure an' there can't be a shadow of a doubt about the legality of our claim to the Ohio strip. But without a voice in Congress, we can't take it to court. We've got Lucius Lyon in Washington, but a Territorial delegate can't vote."

"But I protest that this Constitutional Convention and the elections are all illegal!" Mr. Watling said vehemently.

"Throw him out!" one man demanded.

"Go on back to Detroit! Or to Ohio, if you like it better there."

"I'm a property owner in this county of Hillsdale and I have a right to be heard here," Mr. Watling challenged.

"Sure an' yer a property owner," came the bitter retort. "That we all know."

Anne's heart began to beat wildly. This was more exciting than any Town Meeting she had ever heard about.

"Are you for Mason and Michigan, or agin us?" Mr. Watling was asked.

"Throw him out!" came the demand again.

Papa rose to his feet and Anne caught her breath as she saw all eyes turn to him. What was he going to say? He couldn't take sides with Mr. Watling! But he'd never been for Governor Mason. "Hotspur Governor" he'd called him, back in Detroit. It would be dreadful if he said that now.

Papa's voice was calm and pleasant when he spoke.

"Gentlemen, you're all guests in my house. Let's not talk of throwing anyone out," he said. "The night is warm, I admit. We mustn't let our tempers get the same way."

There was a murmur of assent and a few men laughed. Anne breathed deeply with relief.

"Let's get back to the constitution," Mr. Doyle urged. "Reverend Pierce, will you tell us about that, now."

So Mr. Pierce explained that the Michigan constitution established the schools as a distinct branch of the government. This state — which was not a state — proposed to give one section of land in every sixteen for the support of primary schools. An iron-clad law it was, he said, and his eyes gleamed with the zeal of a crusader. The state would own this land. There would be a State Department of Education and a State Superintendent of Schools. No other state in the Union had such strong provisions for the education of its people. Michigan would have a state university that would be the greatest in America, and its school system would be the best in the world!

"Let the school house and the church be planted as they ever have been in every village and hamlet throughout the length and breadth of our land, and no tyrant can ever arise that can be strong enough to trample or tread down the rights of the people," he shouted, and the men and women in the room were silent before the power of his voice.

Anne's eyes did not leave his face as he talked. His ardor held everyone. His beliefs became theirs.

"The stability of government and the perpetuation of the state depend on the intelligence of the citizens. We must educate, or forge bars and bolts and chains!"

"Nate," Anne whispered, and dug her fingers into his bony knee in her intensity.

"I will, I will teach school!"

But before Nate could answer, there was a sound of a horse's hooves in the yard. A heavy step at the door, and a stranger was standing in the room.

"Men!" he shouted, waving a paper in his hand. "I come by order of General Joseph Brown. Governor Lucas of Ohio has ordered a meeting of his Common Pleas Court in our city of Toledo on September 7th. By that act, he would establish legal claim to our city. Governor Mason has called out the Territorial Militia. We march at once on Toledo! All who haven't joined the militia, join now!"

Yells and cheers followed the tense silence of the moment before. Men crowded about the officer who stood in the doorway with his manifesto. Anne saw her father talking to Reverend Pierce and shaking his hand. She saw the minister write something on a slip of paper and give it to Papa. Then she saw Uncle Luther and Nate moving to join the group of men who were about to be sworn in.

Nate! Were they going to let Nate go? He wasn't seventeen. And Papa? What would he do?

Anne could scarcely breathe for excitement. In the bedlam of cheers and shouting it was hard to think at all. But Governor Mason had ordered the Michigan militia to march on Toledo. This was war!

"You Whigs! Watling, what are you going to do?" There was an ugly tone in the voice that asked the question. Then Papa was standing on a chair, and the clamor subsided a little.

"This is no time to quarrel among ourselves," he said and his voice was clear and forceful. "We are all Michigan men. There is only one issue before us now. Shall we meekly allow more of our land to be taken from us? I for one would rather fight and lose than not protest at all."

"You're right!" and "We'll show 'em!" came the answer as Papa stepped down. He moved through the excited, shoving men who were lining up in front of the officer, until he stood beside Nate and Uncle Luther.

"Raise your right hand," the officer shouted above the din.

Papa and Uncle Luther and Nate were sworn in, along with many others.

CHAPTER

6

Waiting Out the War

Even the wild animals seemed to know the men had gone to war, leaving their womenfolk alone. Partridge and woodcock strutted boldly across the tavern yard, and wild turkeys gobbled and clucked at Anne as she carried water from the well to the kitchen, or hung out the endless wash. For the emigrant wagons continued coming to the tavern nightly, just as though Governor Mason had not sent his call for men to every crossroads hamlet and Tamarack town in Michigan.

The stage coach always stopped at Jonesville. It did not stop at the settlement unless a passenger was getting off, or the driver was flagged down. When Anne saw the coach come to a halt in front of the tavern a few days after Papa left, she groaned. Someone to be under foot the rest of the day, asking questions, wanting this and that, and with so much work to be done!

The passenger alighted and the driver handed a satchel

down to her. Even before she turned toward the tavern, Anne recognized her. Susan Williams! What was she doing at the settlement at this time? Anne dropped a wet towel back into the wash basket and stood beside the clothesline staring in disbelief. It was indeed Susan. Daintily she picked her way across the yard, holding her skirt in one gloved hand, her satchel in the other. Anne looked down at her own wet calico wrapper, and pushed the loose strands of hair back out of her face. What a state to be in when her first friend in Michigan chose to pay her a visit!

Susan did not see her, and went directly to the front door of the tavern. That gave Anne a chance to slip into the kitchen and tidy up a bit before she went into the big room of the inn where she could hear Polly talking to their guest. Anne was still standing before the mirror that hung above the kitchen wash bench when Polly came for her.

"Anne, I've a surprise for you," Polly said.

"I know. I saw her," Anne answered. "And how I look!"

"It isn't just that she's here, so unexpectedly," Polly said. "It's — " and she hesitated.

There was something apprehensive in that unfinished sentence. Anne put the comb back in the wooden box under the mirror and turned to face Polly.

"It's what?" Anne asked. Then, almost in panic, "Has anything happened to Papa? Is anything wrong?"

"No. No, nothing's wrong," Polly replied, but the

nervous way she fingered the folds of her full, flounced skirt told Anne all was not right.

"What is it, Polly, Ma'am?" Anne asked.

"She's come to teach the school, Anne," Polly told her. "Your father engaged her when he got to Detroit, she tells me. Before he left with the militia for Toledo. He told her to come here and you'd take her to Mrs. Doyle's. She's to board there the first week."

For a moment Anne stared at Polly in speechless amazement. Susan Williams had come to teach the school! Papa had hired her!

Anne turned and walked out of the kitchen into the empty yard. The waving towels and sheets on the clothesline blurred before her eyes, and the blood pounded in her temples. She gripped the clothespole with both hands and dug her finger nails into the soft birch bark in disappointment and unreasoning fury.

For a few moments Polly let her stand there. Then she came to Anne's side.

"I knew it would be like this, Anne," she said and her voice choked a little when she spoke. "I can't say anything that will help, either. But you've got to go through with it as he'd expect you to do. You know that."

Slowly Anne loosened her grip on the clothespole. She would, indeed, have to go through with it.

"Go upstairs and change your dress," Polly urged. "By the time you've tidied up a bit you'll be able to hide your feelings."

Numbly Anne nodded. There wasn't anything else

she could do. She couldn't let Susan know how she felt. It was bad enough that Polly knew. But Anne hadn't said anything to reveal her bitterness and she wouldn't. This was what Polly wanted. Someone else to teach the school. Well enough Anne remembered that conversation with Mr. Doyle: "I do wish you'd get a teacher. A good teacher." She could hear Polly's voice again, now.

Without answering, Anne went into the house and up the stairs to her room. She'd change her dress and come down stairs smiling, and take Susan to the Doyles', but never would she go to that school!

That grim decision served to fortify Anne and steadied her when she went to greet Susan, and Susan with her impersonal friendliness, made the meeting easy.

"I was so glad when your father offered me the position," she told Anne while they walked the short distance from the tavern to Mr. Doyle's home. "I didn't know where I might have to go in order to get a school to teach."

"But how did Papa find you?" Anne asked. "I still don't understand what happened."

"He had a letter to Mr. Kirkland, I think. Mr. and Mrs. Kirkland run the Female Seminary in Detroit. A Mr. Pierce wrote the letter. Something like that, anyway."

Anne understood then. She had seen Reverend Pierce give Papa a slip of paper the night of the Hustings.

"I didn't know you were planning to be a teacher, Susan," Anne said.

"You didn't ask me anything about my plans, so how could you know?" Susan smiled. "You were so upset because you'd lost that letter. Remember?"

Anne laughed at the recollection. "That letter didn't matter at all, the way it turned out. We had to stay on the boat, of course. So I'll ask you about yourself now."

"There isn't much to tell and it isn't altogether a gay story," Susan replied. "We've always lived in Detroit. Papa was a surveyor and my brother Franklin's a surveyor too. About a year ago Papa was taken sick and he hasn't been able to get about since, much less do any work. Franklin and I both had to work, so I've been going to the Female Seminary learning to be a teacher, and Mother's a seamstress now."

It wasn't a gay story for a fact, but Susan didn't make a tragedy of what had happened. She was just going ahead, doing the thing that seemed logical and best. And she such a little thing, holding her new bonnet on her head with one hand as she picked her way along the rutted Turnpike, stepping high over logs and watching carefully lest she slip into a mudhole.

"Is Franklin older than you?" Anne asked. She supposed he must be.

"Just a year. He'd have come with me to see how I'll be situated, only he belongs to the Militia and had to go to Toledo. Franklin's been right wonderful," she added proudly. "He's had to be head of the family this past year."

"I'm sure you're all a wonderful family," Anne told her with honest admiration. It was impossible not to like Susan.

"I suppose they'll want me to start the school tomorrow," Susan said inquiringly as Anne pointed out the Doyle house just ahead. "You'll be there, of course."

Anne looked to the side of the road. Wild grapes and rust-topped sumach splashed the clearing with color.

"With no one to do the work at the tavern except my step-mother, who's been sick all summer, and Aunt Ellen and me — " she shook her head. "I should be gathering these grapes for jell right now. The little Crawfords will be there, though."

"I can understand about the work well enough," Susan agreed. "Only you should come to school."

Susan did not press the point nor pry further into Anne's concerns. She was just as Anne remembered her; a placid little person with problems and interests of her own to think about.

Anne was glad when they reached the Doyle yard. Missing the job at the school was something she couldn't talk about, to Susan or Mrs. Doyle or anyone. She said goodbye to Susan quickly and at once started back to the tavern.

Neither Polly nor Aunt Ellen said anything to Anne about going to school, but they looked at her inquiringly and she was sure they had discussed it when she was not around. However, they did indeed need her at the tavern. The food supply was melting away, for one thing. Beans and the wild vetch and dried apple pie had been all they could serve one night. Somebody must make a trip to the mill for flour and corn meal. And where was her Indian friend, Baw Beese? Couldn't he be depended upon to supply them with venison and wild-foul? Or must the women kill the game themselves? Baw Beese had disappeared with the rest of the men in Michigan.

Anne hitched the horses to the buckboard and started for the mill early. Perhaps she would come upon Baw Beese or some of his band along the road. But they were nowhere to be seen, and when she reached the mill it was closed. A farm wife with a load of corn was sitting on her wagon seat, staring in dismay at the empty building.

"There's no flour or meal to be had at the store in Jonesville either," she told Anne. "I've been there already. Their supplies is awful skimpy."

"I wouldn't know how to start the mill going if we could break in, would you?" Anne asked.

"We couldn't break in with just our bare hands," the woman told her.

"If I only knew where that Baw Beese is," Anne wailed. "He'd know how to grind corn, I'm sure. We've got to grind it ourselves. How else are we to eat? You'll sell me some of yours, won't you?"

The farmer's wife brightened. She had seen Baw Beese back down the road a bit, and the Indians surely knew how to grind corn without a mill. She would sell part of her load to Anne, too.

Together they followed the Turnpike until they came to a crossroads and a clearing where the Indians were camped.

"Baw Beese, how did people grind corn before there were grist mills?" Anne asked. "You should know."

"Grind corn in hollow oak stump," he told her. "You want to grind corn? Come."

He led them back to a spot near Jonesville where sapling trees and a thinning of the brush at the edge of the forest gave evidence of an abandoned clearing.

Baw Beese motioned them to follow him. "First settlers ground corn here. Before grist mill," he said.

Anne looked at the crude mills with a sinking heart. Two oak stumps they were, with a hollow made by burning a hole in the top. A stick about six feet long and eight inches in diameter, and rounded at the bottom, was hung by a spring pole over each stump.

The farmer's wife gave one look at the stumps and began cleaning out the accumulation of dirt and leaves.

"We may as well be at it," she said. "We can clean the stumps with corn cobs. Then we can start."

"White man say he pound peck of dry corn into meal in half hour," Baw Beese said, but he did not offer to do any of the work himself.

"White women will take longer," Anne told him. "But thanks for finding the place for us, Baw Beese. And promise to bring venison to the tavern tomorrow, will you?"

"Twenty-five cent pound," Baw Beese replied.

That was the price the Indians charged, Anne knew. Polly would be glad to pay it. They must have meat of some kind.

The rough pole soon blistered Anne's hands and her back ached from bending, but she pounded the pestle up and down, grinding the golden kernels against the hard oak bowl. She was getting corn meal, and with johnny cake and venison on the table, who had a right to complain? So she pounded on, up and down, all the rest of the day.

It was almost supper time when Anne got back to the tavern. Luther and Lucy had been watching for her and she heard them shout to Aunt Ellen and Polly when she drove the wagon around the bend and into sight. Then they ran to meet her and climbed onto the buckboard from the back, where there was no danger from horses' hooves or wheels.

"You'll have johnny cake for certain now," Anne promised them. "I ground this meal for you myself."

"*Merci*," said Luther with a mischievous smile.

"*Merci beaucoup*," Lucy said saucily.

"What?" Anne asked.

"*Merci beaucoup*," the twins repeated. Then in laughing sing-song, "Anne doesn't know. Anne doesn't know what it means."

And Anne didn't. "So you tell me," she said.

"It means 'thank you' in French," they explained proudly and in the same breath. "The new teacher taught us. We're going to learn one French word every day."

French! So Susan Williams would teach them French like the old school law said she should.

Anne told herself that she didn't care. Her hands were smarting and her muscles ached, and she had eaten nothing except a few wild raspberries since breakfast. All she wanted was some supper and a chance to crawl into bed. Let Susan teach them Greek if she wanted to!

Baw Beese did not come with the venison until the next night, and then he drove a bargain. It had rained all day, a horrid drizzle, and the air was cold enough for snow. The fireplaces at the tavern were ablaze with logs and the guests were crowded around their cheering warmth.

"Injun cold," Baw Beese said when Polly opened the kitchen door in response to his knock. "Squaw cold. Papoose cold. Stay night here."

"But Baw Beese, the tavern's full of people. There's no room," Polly protested.

"Injun bring venison, but Injun stay inside tonight," Baw Beese repeated.

"Let them sleep here in the kitchen," Anne suggested. "There's plenty of room. The guests don't need to know they're here." Then turning to the Indians: "You'd just as soon sleep in the kitchen as anywhere, wouldn't you?"

Baw Beese, two squaws, three other braves, and four Indian children pushed past Polly, who looked at Anne in despair.

Baw Beese produced the venison and Polly paid him. Then as Anne brought out baked beans and johnny cake, he took a pouch from one of the squaws and poured bright red cranberries onto the table.

"You Injun's friend," he said to Anne. "First red berries Injuns get. Come long way from lakes. No red berries here."

Anne knew she had not seen any cranberries in the clearings or marshes near the settlement. There was no knowing where Baw Beese and his followers might have wandered in the sparsely settled lake country.

With the tart cranberries and venison and wild honey, Anne made mincemeat and stored it away for winter. She gathered the first hickory nuts and walnuts that fell from the trees, and bitter wild grapes for jelly. Each day she watched the Turnpike and listened for the sound of Papa's voice, singing as he came home. For word had come out from Detroit that the war ended ten days after it started, and without a shot fired. So many different stories reached the settlement that Anne had no idea what the right of it might be. But Papa would stop in Detroit to take care of his business before he came home, she knew. Dull, work-filled weeks might pass before he came.

CHAPTER 7

They Called it "Victory"

It was Uncle Luther who came home first from the Ohio war, but little time he had to tell the women folk about it. Papa had lined up a sizeable hauling business, and new shipments of goods had come in from the East. He needed his peddler's wagon and his heavy Conestoga wagon right away. Uncle Luther and Anne must drive the wagons back to Detroit, with as little delay as possible.

"But Nate?" Aunt Ellen and Anne asked in the same breath. "Where's Nate?"

"I hadn't the heart to make him come home," Uncle Luther admitted. "The lad who was Governor Mason's orderly at the Ohio War was took sick. Nate has his place for a little spell, and so proud he is! I hadn't the heart."

After that, Anne could scarcely wait to get to Detroit. Nate an orderly for Stevens Thompson Mason! Speaking to him every day! Perhaps she would see the Governor again. Perhaps he would speak to her, too.

It was dusk when they reached the outskirts of the capital, but even in the dimming light, Anne could sense restlessness and tension. Rigs of all kinds were hurrying past them toward the heart of the city. Two-wheeled carts and fancier cabriolets skirted between heavier, slower vehicles. Men and women jostled each other on the wooden sidewalks. Dogs barked, and shouting children dashed in front of the peddler's wagon.

Houses and stores on either side of the street were brightly lighted. In the wavering halos Anne could see crêpe hanging over many doorways. Strangely out of place the black cloth seemed in a city agog with excitement, and she was at a loss to understand it. Ahead, lighted flares zig-zagged dizzily as though a parade were in progress. Anne had her hands full managing the horses, suddenly become nervous and skittish. She held the reins tightly to keep them close behind Uncle Luther. He made his way through the congestion to the Steamboat Hotel and there turned both rigs over to a stableman.

At the door of the hotel Anne hesitated. Where was Nate? Somehow she had expected he would be waiting to greet her, but he was nowhere in sight. And what of her appearance? The sidewalk, the steps, and the rooms inside were all crowded with people.

Anne adjusted the green and brown velvet bonnet Polly had made for her and was thankful for the Lady's Book which kept her abreast of the fashions. Her dark brown coat was well designed and the material good, she knew. Papa's merchandise was of the best. She had a comfortable feeling about her clothes when Uncle Luther led her into the crowded diningroom.

Papa did not see them at once. He was seated at a large table, surrounded by other men, and clearly he was engaged in an argument. His first words, and the tone in which he spoke, chilled Anne's spirits.

"But we had sober-minded men in Washington who counselled Mason against this move," she heard him say sharply. "Lucius Lyon, for one."

There was no mistaking Papa's meaning. He had gone to the war for Michigan, but he still was questioning the leadership of the Boy Governor.

"True enough, Rogers," a young man answered, and there was irritation in his voice too. "Mason knew all that. He didn't think caution was the move which would save the Ohio strip for Michigan, or get us into the Union either."

Uncle Luther interrupted them then, and the next minute Papa's strong arm was around Anne's shoulders.

"Well, Franklin, here's another devotee of your hero," he said. "Anne, this is Susan Williams' brother, Franklin. As blind a Mason worshipper as yourself."

Franklin Williams rose to acknowledge the introduction. Six feet tall he was, and all bone and muscle. His face and neck were tanned to an Indian brown, and his long, blond hair, brushed back in the fashion the Governor followed, seemed white against his high forehead. His eyes were blue and his brows heavy and dark, giving him an altogether arresting appearance. But even the heavy tan did not quite hide the flush that met her father's words. He ran his long fingers nervously across the back of his chair, and it seemed to Anne that the look he gave her was penetrating and his attitude distant. As another Mason follower, and Susan's friend, she would have expected a warmer greeting from Franklin Williams. It must be that Papa's feeling against the Governor was keeping this surprisingly attractive young man standing so formally behind his chair.

Papa, however, seemed not to notice it. "This is Oscar Kruger," he said, indicating a boy of about Anne's age or perhaps a little older. "Oscar is coming out to the settlement with us. He thinks there should be some Germans in the Irish Hills. How about it, Oscar?"

Papa laughed his own, whole-hearted laugh, and the tension eased.

Oscar, Anne noted, was a strapping youth and ruddy-faced, with hair cropped short. It was hard to tell what color it might be. Light, with a reddish cast it seemed in the lamplight.

"Last of all, this is Dr. Brown," Papa continued. "A neighbor of ours out on the Turnpike and a level-headed man."

The stout, slightly bald doctor acknowledged the introduction with a smile and the men sat down again. Anne drew her own chair close to her father's side.

"We've just been having a little argument about going to another 'Victory Dinner'," Papa admitted lightly, patting Anne's arm as he spoke. "This last 'Victory Dinner' seemed like one too many for me."

"Then we won?" Anne asked eagerly.

"We were completely licked!" Papa said emphatically. "Your fine Boy Governor was removed from office by President Jackson and the Michigan militia was disbanded and told to go home. But Michigan just won't admit defeat. We're calling it a victory."

Astounded, Anne looked from her father to Franklin Williams.

"I thought President Jackson was a friend of the Mason family," Anne said in bewilderment. "He appointed Stevens Thompson as our Territorial Secretary and then Governor. How could he do this now?"

"Jackson's still on our side, I believe. But he had to do it, Miss Rogers," Franklin said. He glanced at her again, and she saw the same questioning look in his eyes, before he went on with his explanation. "The Ohio bloc and the votes they control in Congress forced him to do it. Mason was warned of that, as your father said. But he forced the issue. He made them all show their hands. He'd have won a decision in the Supreme Court if he could have carried the dispute there. And his militia kept the Ohio forces out of Michigan territory too, until he was removed. That was the only way they could defeat him."

Franklin, Anne realized, was a very different person from his sister. There was an impersonal air about Susan. The affairs of others did not move her too much. That Franklin felt deeply about Mason was evident from his strained look and the emotion in his voice. The Michigan situation was more on his mind than the advent of a strange young lady, Anne was sure, yet he had looked at her as though there was something more he wanted to say or know.

Franklin's intensity carried to all in the group. Only Papa held out against him.

"Some militia we were," Papa ridiculed. "Twelve hundred backwoodsmen marching against the great state of Ohio with its million free men. Muskets or rifles or shotguns over our shoulders and cooking utensils hanging at our sides. No uniforms, of course." He laughed then at his own description and the memory of the Michigan militia.

"But Mason had three loaded transports out in the Toledo harbor, and Lucas had only five hundred men assembled," Franklin insisted, leaning forward in his intensity. "The Ohio boys weren't so eager to fight us, you'll admit. They stayed in Perrysburg, didn't they?"

"And you'll admit they outsmarted us, won't you?" Papa asked in turn. Then he explained the maneuver to Anne.

"Lucas ordered a session of an Ohio court held in Toledo, to establish a legal claim to the strip, remember?" he asked. "Well, an Ohio judge and a bailiff and a couple of others slipped into Toledo about midnight one night and held a session of their court in an empty building. They wrote out all their records and about three o'clock in the morning they slipped back across the line without our knowing about it."

Anne looked at Franklin. He was staring at his hands and did not dispute her father's statement.

"Meantime our militia went on drilling, and yelling taunts at the Ohio militia, and eating the farmers out of house and home," Papa continued. "It was a great war and everybody was having a good time until a messenger rode out from Detroit with the news of Mason's removal. That stopped our dress parade."

Again Anne looked at Franklin, but before he could speak the room rocked to the sound of a booming cannon. Papa lay a reassuring hand on Anne's trembling arm.

"Mason must be coming," he said. "Detroit hung out crêpe to greet the new governor President Jackson sent us. He was met by a funeral wagon! Every time Mason appears on the streets the guns go off in salute. Don't feel too bad about his defeat, Anne. He's the most spectacular figure in the United States today. He's brought Michigan's cause before the whole country. I'll grant him that."

"I'm glad to hear you say it, Rogers," Franklin spoke up and he looked steadily into Papa's eyes, and unflinchingly. "We're going to elect him Governor and adopt his Constitution too. The President and the whole United States government will know in another month that Mason rules Michigan, and not that pudgy stooge Jackson sent out to replace him."

Papa shook his head.

"Give Mason a little more maturity, Frank," he urged. "He's a leader and a powerhouse, I'll admit. Give him a few more years before you elect him Governor."

Anne struggled to keep her silence. How could Papa be so against Governor Mason? It was unbelievable that

Papa should not be on her side. On Governor Mason's side. How could she ever expect him to let her teach in the Governor's great school program if he felt Mason had been wrong? Not mature enough to govern the state, Papa thought. That had been his reason for not letting her teach the settlement school, too.

Anne wanted to speak up, but how could she speak against her own father! All the excitement and joy of the trip to Detroit began to fade. Never before had she felt apart from Papa.

Then Dr. Brown entered the conversation and Anne knew at once that here was another Mason follower.

"You do him an injustice, Rogers," Dr. Brown said. "Now is the time for us to support Mason. You've just seen him risk his political future for Michigan. I've seen him risk his very life, day after day, for the people of this Territory."

"When?" Anne asked, forgetting her intent to keep silent. "How?" Clearly this quiet-speaking physician knew more than anyone else at the table.

"In 1832 in the cholera epidemic," Dr. Brown related. "A wheezing old side-wheeler named the *Henry Clay* brought the disease to Detroit. In the early summer it was. A month later Detroit was a pestilence-ridden death hole."

"I recall it," Franklin said. "We were all here."

"Tonight you'd never know this was the same city," Dr. Brown continued. "Stores and warehouses stood open and deserted then, for the owners dropped dead without warning. Thieves didn't dare venture inside to pilfer. Funeral bells tolled all day. Carts went through the city at night with bells ringing, for people to drag out their dead. Pitch pine knots were burning day and night on street corners and in alleys, because some fools thought the black, stinking smoke would drive out the disease."

Anne shuddered at the description.

"That was when Mason showed the stuff he's made of," Dr. Brown went on, carefully avoiding Papa's eyes, and staring into the crowded tables beyond them. "He was the one who rallied all the courageous souls and helped them get organized. Went with them to distribute food and medicine. When the villages out-state got terrified, he it was who tore down the barricades they set up to block the roads leading to Detroit. Roads had to be kept open so food and medicine could get through. You'd see him galloping along the Turnpike day and night, coat-tails flying behind him and his high hat plunked down on his head. Just a long-legged boy defying gun barrels to tear down those blockades and save the people who were still alive. Or stopping to help a country doc like me."

No one spoke for a time after Dr. Brown finished his story. Anne swallowed hard. How could Papa still feel that Mason was not the man to govern Michigan? She glanced up at him. His face was thoughtful and he seemed about to speak, but at that moment men at the tables nearest the door broke into a song. Soon the entire room was a bedlam of excited cheers and voices calling "Mason!" People climbed onto their chairs and shouted. The song was taken up by everyone.

"Old Lucas gave his orders for all to hold a court
　But Stevens Thompson Mason, he thought he'd have
　　some sport.
He called upon the Wolverines and asked them for to go
　To meet the rebel Lucas, his court to overthrow."

The verses seemed innumerable. Anne stood on tiptoe and looked toward the door. Mason must be there, in that surging, singing crowd. She would see him again.

And indeed she did. Close behind him came Nate, eyes shining and scrubbed face beaming. Never had she seen old sober-sides Nate looking so happy.

Slowly the Governor made his way from table to table, speaking to those he knew. His eyes were searching the room, and at last he caught sight of Franklin. Anne saw the look of recognition that passed between the two young men, and her heart raced. He was coming toward them now. To their table. Governor Mason and her own cousin Nate!

Proudly Franklin made the introductions and Governor Mason shook hands with all, bowing politely to Anne. He paused as Franklin presented Papa.

"I recall your face well," the Governor said, "but the occasion escapes me."

"You have many faces to remember, Sir," Papa replied but he did not mention the day when first he and the Governor had met. Mason paused, then turned to Franklin and gripped his hand for a moment.

Nate slipped quietly to Anne's side. There was a knowing look on his face when his eyes met hers, and she was proud to have him standing beside her chair. Glad to know that he, too, was loyal to Mason. But he said nothing now, and with the others waited for the Governor to speak or act.

"I couldn't go without saying good bye to you, Frank," Mason said quietly. "I'm leaving in the morning."

"Leaving!" Franklin exclaimed. "No! For where?"

"I'm going to New York," the Governor answered. "It wouldn't be right for me to stay here and embarrass Governor Horner any longer."

"Governor Horner!" Franklin fairly snorted. "He's not governor of Michigan and never will be. Michigan won't have him."

With a quick gesture Mason pushed back his long, dark hair. He was wearing the high white collar and black neck-stock Anne remembered, but his dress was more informal than it had been the day she saw him leaving the capitol building. There was a casualness about him now as he mingled with the people he had so lately governed. Without the starched lace ruffles at his wrists, without the gold-handled cane and high silk hat, he was less the dignitary. Here was the man the people loved.

"I'm fearful that you're right, Frank," he said. Then, lowering his voice, "When Horner went to the capitol building he couldn't even find his office. Workmen were changing signs and moving desks and file cabinets around. Nobody would speak to him, much less answer his questions. He finally had to come to me for help. That wasn't pleasant for him."

"What did you do?" Franklin asked.

"I took him back to the capitol and introduced him to his staff," Mason said with a wry smile. "I'm afraid he's in for trouble. He thinks he can force Michigan to fall in line now. He doesn't know us, Frank. His ideas aren't going to set well with our people."

"All the more reason why you can't leave Michigan now," Franklin argued. "It — it might be misunderstood."

"There's nothing to misunderstand," Mason replied and his face sobered. "While I was Governor, I executed the laws of the Territory. I believed we had both the law and the right of it, on our side. But Ohio had the political power we lacked. Now I submit to my fate and am even satisfied with the result."

Speechlessly the group at the table heard his decision. Nate leaned over Anne's chair and whispered in her ear. "When I bring him his horse tomorrow, it will be the last time I'll ever do it, but he'll be back and don't you fear!"

Governor Mason turned from Franklin to shake hands with the men in his group. Anne trembled as she curtsied in acknowledging his bow. When he left the hotel, the crowd followed him. Only a few knew of his plans; a stunned silent group unable now to participate in the lusty cheers or to join in the half-hysterical torch light parade through the streets.

When Nate left her to follow the Governor, Anne looked at Susan's brother. A determined look had hardened his strong, even features. Dr. Brown was wiping his glasses, slowly and repeatedly. There was no smile on

Papa's face and he was staring at the crowd without seeming to see anyone at all. Finally he turned to Franklin and spoke slowly.

"You were right, Franklin," he said. "You and the doctor and all the rest. Now is the time for Michigan to stand back of Mason, come what may."

A tear spilled from Anne's eyes, but it was a tear of relief and happiness. With Papa on their side, it seemed that Mason couldn't lose! She wanted to shout it aloud.

But just what were these men going to do now? How were they going to repay Mason? How save him?

CHAPTER 8

And the Woods Echoed "Mason!"

Polling places were set up in every township and the people of Michigan swarmed to their crossroads churches and schools in buckboards and on horseback. At the settlement, Anne watched as sunbonneted women with crocks of flavorful baked beans and pans of johnny cake arrived with their men. No proclamation had been issued, but the election of Stevens Thompson Mason was a two-day holiday throughout the state. Bonfires blazed and drums beat and the woods echoed the shout of "Mason! Mason!" He received 7,508 votes to 814 for some rival nobody remembered. His constitution was adopted by a vote of 6,229 to 1,359.

The settlement greeted the election returns with fresh outbursts of cheers and another parade. From school to tavern and back again the people marched, flags waving, children racing and shouting, dogs yapping at their heels. Baw Beese and his Indians stood in the clearing, blankets around their shoulders and watched in silence. The October sun was bright. It danced on the red and gold and russet and green of the trees, and the wind whipped Anne's red wool scarf about like a banner while she fairly danced along the Turnpike.

"And what are you Whigs going to do now?" Mr. Doyle taunted Mr. Watling.

"We're going to call a party caucus. We'll declare this action illegal until Michigan has the consent of the U. S. Congress," Mr. Watling replied.

"Go ahead and caucus," Mr. Doyle said with an impudent grin.

"It's absolutely illegal!" Mr. Watling shouted. "It shatters all precedent. Holding an election! Naming a Governor! Adopting a constitution, and we're not even a state!"

"But Mason's Governor of Michigan just the same," Mr. Doyle replied jubilantly. "That's our answer to Governor Lucas and President Jackson, too!"

"It's an audacious insult to the President," Mr. Watling stormed. "Do you think we're going to get into the Union by holding a gun at the Congress?"

Mr. Doyle ignored the question. The crowd was with him and against Mr. Watling.

"Sure and next month he'll be inaugurated," he said. "Detroit'll put on a show the like of which the whole country can envy."

"Oh, I wish I could be there!" Susan exclaimed. "Mr. Doyle, can't the inauguration be a school holiday?"

"Why not?" he replied. "There's no Whigs on the school board!"

Susan squeezed Anne's hand. "You can come with me," she said. "You and Nate both. I'll send word to Franklin and he'll see that we all get invited to everything. He'll have a partner for Nate and an escort for me and we'll go everywhere!"

Anne could not recall ever seeing Susan so excited. She must indeed have missed the capital city and her friends there, much more than anyone at the settlement had realized. The inauguration would be a home-coming for Susan, and the parties more important than anything the Governor might say, Anne surmised. She wondered about Susan's friends and her life before she came to the settlement, as her thoughts raced ahead to the great event and to Franklin. He had not paid much heed to her the night she had met him in Detroit, but he had been on her mind often since then. Well she recalled the sun-bronzed features, the slim figure, and the intense blue eyes. To know him and talk with him would be almost like knowing the Governor himself. She had asked Susan about Franklin once when she saw her friend receiving letters from home.

"He's too intense about everything," Susan said. "First it was his surveying. He practically slept with his tripod. Now its politics and Governor Mason."

Anne had glanced questioningly at the letters then, and now she recalled what Susan had said. "They aren't all from Franklin. There's a special friend who writes to me. He's away in New York studying at the Columbia

School of Medicine. But he writes." She had smiled with satisfaction when she said it.

"Susan, will your friend be home for the inauguration?" Anne asked now. "The one who's away at medical school? That would make it such wonderful fun for you."

Susan shook her head. "He couldn't come all the way from New York," Susan told Anne. "I know all of Franklin's friends, though. He'll find someone free to escort me. And we'll have fun, don't you fear."

Anne was sure of it. Now she would have an opportunity to get acquainted with Franklin, and there was the certainty that she would see the Governor once more. She might even meet him, for she would be at the inauguration with Susan and Franklin.

Even Nate's sober features lighted at the invitation. He had talked of little except the Governor since his return from the Ohio war — the Governor and the black horse he rode.

"Maybe there'll be snow by November," he said. "I'll get my sleigh finished and we can drive to Detroit in that. It's going to be fast and light. I wish the Governor could see it."

"Nate designed it himself," Anne told Susan as the three walked back to the Tavern. "He measured every board. The body's of oak and the runners are ash."

"It's beautiful," Susan said when she saw it. "But why the different woods, Nate?"

"Ash bends better than oak," Nate explained with a show of indifference, trying to hide his pride in the sleigh and his pleasure at the girls' praise. "The runners had to bend up, so they're of ash. This sleigh will be real fast."

"I hope there'll be ice on the river, or at least on the low marshes along side," Susan said. "If there is, you must enter the races, Nate."

"What races?" Anne and Nate inquired in the same breath.

"All the young men in Detroit race in the winter," Susan explained. "Older men, too. It's quite the sport of the Detroit Young Men's Society. Franklin belongs and so does Governor Mason. It's a right pretty sight to see the cabriolets skimming over the ice, their bells tinkling and all. Governor Mason often comes to watch."

"And Nate could race?" Anne asked excitedly. "He could race before the Governor? The Detroit Young Men's Society isn't too exclusive for us?"

"They don't own the river or the races," Susan said. "Anyway, Franklin belongs. Nate can race, of course."

Anne did not try to conceal her exuberance. Governor Mason at the races, and Nate racing with the best of them! Winning, perhaps. The Governor would be there at the finish line, as she imagined it, and she would be there too, with Franklin. She could picture it all — the straining horses, the cheering crowds, the Governor greeting the winner. Then in the evening, the ball.

"Oh, Susan," she said in sudden panic. "I'm sure people don't dance at balls in Detroit the way we do out here. You'll teach us to dance, won't you? And what about our manners?"

"Your manners are all right," Susan said. "And I'll teach you the dances if you'll come to school as you should." Then turning to Polly who had joined them at the shed, "There's no need for Anne to stay out of school longer, is there, Polly?"

Anne flushed at the mention of school. More than once recently she had thought about that determination, made in anger a few short weeks ago. Well she knew it had been wrong, and she had wondered why no one had questioned it. Quickly she glanced at Polly who was running a hand along Nate's sleigh, her face turned from the girls.

"Sister Ellen and I can manage now, I think, if Anne wants to come to a bargain with you, Susan," was all Polly had to say.

"You'll have to learn the schottische and quadrille and the minuet. You'll need an evening dress too," Susan warned Anne.

They were making it easy for her, Anne realized. There was only one sensible thing to do, too. She hoped that her voice would not sound too unnatural, and that no one would look at her reddened cheeks when she replied.

"I've got to learn the dances, of course," she said, trying to make it appear that the party alone mattered. "I wonder if Papa has any of that pink material left. The ladies along the Turnpike have much admired the fine cottons and woolens that are being manufactured in the mills of New York State and Pennsylvania, Papa told me. The brocades and laces too."

But Polly had a different idea and as they walked together to the house, she mentioned it.

"He had some sage green brocade," she said thoughtfully. "It was a much richer piece of goods and more unusual. Almost any brunette can wear pink, but you have the coloring for that sage green, Anne."

Anne wanted to protest. Polly had just won one point.

"I thought green was for an older person," she reasoned. "Now the pink — "

"An older person couldn't carry it off the way you can," Polly said with a note of finality as she led the way into the big room and found the Lady's Book. "Here. Here's how we'll make it," she said.

Anne was ready to object again. She hadn't even been given a chance to look at the fashions. But when she saw the dress Polly had chosen to pattern, she caught her breath in delight. It was cut low and square across front and back to expose the shoulders. Melon sleeves, ballooning to the elbows, were caught in a band of lace. The close-fitting bodice was lace-trimmed too, and the full, ankle-length skirt was entirely unadorned. Nothing would detract from the rich pattern in the brocade.

"You'll come to your sixteenth birthday just after the inauguration," Polly commented. "This will be a fitting party dress for a young girl of sixteen."

Polly and Aunt Ellen at once began making the pattern and stitching and fitting. With Polly at the melodeon, the dancing lessons started that very evening. In no time at all Anne and Nate had mastered the new steps and learned how to bow and curtsy properly.

"Anne, you'll be the belle of the ball," Susan said at last. "Franklin will be right proud to take you to the party at the Mansion House. That green does something positively electric to the blue of your eyes. And you do have the longest black lashes."

Anne thrilled at the compliments, and the prospect of her first grown-up ball. In this dress certainly Franklin would take note of her. She was glad, too, that the question of school had been settled so easily.

Detroit was crowded with people who had come for the inauguration. Even the big eastern newspapers had sent representatives to cover it, and once more hotels were turning people away. Each home was filled with house guests.

Anne and Nate were cordially welcomed by Susan's plump and smiling mother, her slender father in his invalid's chair, and by Franklin. It was natural, of course, that their first thought should be for Susan. They had not seen her since the school opened at the settlement, and Franklin kept asking her how she was making out . . . was she comfortable . . . was she well treated at the homes where she boarded round.

"And everyone's made you welcome?" he asked with a trace of concern in his voice. "You've had no trouble at the school?"

"It's a wonderful school, just as I wrote you," Susan assured him. "The big boys have started now, but Nate's there to help hold them in line. And the little ones love Anne. Mr. Rogers told us I'd have no trouble, and I've had none."

Franklin, particularly, seemed relieved.

"I have a table reserved for us at the Steamboat Hotel,"

he told Susan and with a smile included Anne and Nate. "I thought our guests would like to see the political figures who are sure to be there. You'll find many of your friends in the crowd, too, Susan."

They were all eager to be off, and Franklin seemed pleased to point out the important people who filled the lobby.

"Mason used to come here almost every night for law instruction until he passed the bar in 1833," Franklin explained to Nate while Anne listened. "He got something of a reputation he didn't deserve because of it. People who didn't know that Kintsing Pritchett was coaching him so he could pass the bar, had much to say about his nightly 'revels' here. It was the same time I was studying to become a surveyor."

Nate nodded and winked knowingly at Franklin, and Anne's mind raced ahead to the social events to follow. Perhaps when he saw her dressed for the ball — .

Franklin had located a vantage point at the commons from which they could watch as the Governor rode to the capitol. He had arranged for them to get into the building and hear the inaugural message, too. He was indeed a thoughtful host, but he was giving Nate more attention than he showed Anne, and she couldn't help a feeling of disappointment.

The *Detroit Gazette* had announced the hour when the inaugural procession would leave the Governor's home on Jefferson Street. Franklin and his guests left early for the capitol grounds, but men and women already lined the route, even though the air was sharp. The Detroit guards had a hard time, in fact, holding back the crowd as the Governor's carriage proceeded along the line of march.

The route led past the homes of the old French settlers where crucifixes hung in front yards, and bare branches of fruit trees shivered against the wintry blue sky. Past the raw new store buildings now pushing north on Woodward Avenue it went, to the capitol grounds.

Men cheered and tossed their stovepipe hats into the air. Ladies waved and laughed and cried at the sight of their Governor. Anne could see them pressing forward from the uneven, wooden sidewalks onto the street, waving and shouting. Long before she could see the procession she could hear excited cries of *"Vive!"* mingling with the lusty cheers of backwoodsmen, and the more polite enthusiasm of Detroit's intelligentsia.

"Mason! Mason!"

At last she saw the cavalry, plumes waving in the chill breeze, crossed belts glistening white against dark uniforms. Then, in an open carriage, came the man who had set a nation talking; the handsome, daring Boy Governor of Michigan, just turned twenty-four years old.

Anne caught her breath at the sight of him. Gone was the casual friendliness she remembered. Here was the hero Michigan acclaimed, the man of bearing that a rough, backwoods state had supported and honored in defiance of the President and the authority of the United States Congress.

He was all that his people expected of him. His black broadcloth evening suit was tight-fitting and superbly tailored. At his wrists starched, white lace ruffles glistened and white silk gloves covered his hands. A wide black satin neck stock circled an even higher collar that held his chin back between stiff, gleaming-white points. From his shoulders hung a white wool blanket with long, twisted silk fringe, the latest fashion in New York. He carried a gold-handled ebony walking stick, and as the people cheered he doffed his high silk hat and bowed with great formality.

Anne glanced at Franklin. His face was tense, and an admiration close to worship burned in his eyes. He raised one hand in salute but he did not cheer.

Anne's feet tingled with cold, for the ground beneath her was frozen, but nothing could have driven her from the scene. After the Governor had entered the capitol building, he reappeared on the portico and brought his administrative staff out with him. Dignified, mature men they were, all properly dressed for the occasion.

Shouts and cheers were punctuated with repeated cries of "We're with you, Boy!"

"Why, there's Reverend Pierce!" Anne exclaimed as she recognized the Marshall minister standing with the Governor's staff.

"He's state superintendent of public instruction, didn't you know?" Franklin said. "Michigan is the first state in the Union to have a state superintendent of schools. Pierce is the very first state superintendent in the whole country. His plan for free primary schools to educate every child, and a great state University, is going through now. That's just one of the things Michigan will have, thanks to Mason!"

"And the Whigs dare to say he's a menace!" Anne cried. "That he's trying to get us into the Union like a bully with a gun."

Bonfires burned in the streets that night and musicians played and impromptu parades started. People crowded the Steamboat Hotel and the Mansion House and the American House. He might appear anywhere. He had always been one to take part in community activities. Franklin Williams and his sister and their guests mingled with the excited crowd, unwilling to go home.

"There'll be a big turn-out for the races tomorrow, Nate," Franklin said. "Are you ready?"

"I haven't seen the other rigs, but I'm ready," Nate replied.

It was the largest crowd ever to gather in Michigan, Susan and Franklin declared enthusiastically when they reached the river the next afternoon.

"Those are fine looking horses and smart sleighs," Anne observed as she watched the men grouped about the starting line. "But I have no fear for you, Nate."

Men and women in fur-lined coats and boots and mittens chatted eagerly while they moved toward the goal, keeping an expectant eye on the road at the same time. Governor Mason loved the races.

Franklin and Susan already had jumped from the sleigh when a shout went up. Mason was coming! Anne and Nate sat in breathless admiration watching him drive past them toward the finish line. He was nodding to right and left, smiling and waving in friendly fashion, yet with the same erect dignity as when he rode to his inaugural. Anne could not keep her eyes from him.

Unexpectedly, while she watched, Nate shoved the reins into her hands.

"There's a man I've just got to see," he said and bounding out of the sleigh he disappeared into the crowd.

Anne took the reins, her eyes still on the Governor who was now well up ahead of her. Not until the starter's shrill call brought her back to reality did she sense that Nate might not be able to take part in the races. Where was he?

Anne stood up in the sleigh, looking in all directions. Where were Susan and Franklin? They, too, had disappeared in the crowd. Someone must find Nate, though! He had to enter the races, and she couldn't leave the horses to search him out.

Once more the starter blew his whistle. The sleighs were lining up on the ice and her own horses, sensing the activity, were pawing the ground and chafing at the bit.

Anne had no time to think. If Nate's sleigh was to enter the races, she would have to drive it. And at the finish line was Michigan's hero! Governor Mason might see her. Might even speak to her if she won!

Anne pulled the tight wool hat down close around her face and flicked the lines on the horses' sleek sides. Adroitly she maneuvered them into position. She was on her knees now, in the front of the sleigh, lines taut, every muscle tense.

The gun sounded. Spectators cheered and yelled from the sidelines. The carioles were off on the ice.

Anne had driven her father's horses ever since she could remember. They knew her and her touch. Other drivers might lay on the whip. Anne had only to flick it lightly and call them by name and urge them on.

Like ringing anvils were the beating hooves on the ice. Carefully she guided her team through one narrow opening between sleighs, then another. She could hear the rasping breathing of drivers and animals as she passed.

She was moving up!

"Go! Go!" she shouted to the horses, calling them by name. "Giddap! Go!"

There was only one sleigh ahead as the goal line loomed before her calculating eyes. She couldn't win, but she might tie. She snapped the whip sharply over the horses' rumps, but a final burst of speed from the lead team cheated her out of any honor but second place.

Anne slid limply back into the seat of the sleigh. She had done her best, but it had not been quite good enough. She must find Nate now. He would be there somewhere, surely. Before she had a chance to look for him, however, men were surrounding her sleigh, exclaiming in surprise, demanding her name.

"A girl? It can't be!"

"Anne Rogers? Where are you from?"

"You should have been the winner! Jehosophat!"

"Carry her to town on your shoulders, boys!"

Anne stood in the sleigh, eager hands reaching out to her, men's faces grinning congratulations.

"The Governor should have stayed for the finish," someone said. "Why need he have hurried back?"

"He came to fetch one of his staff to a meeting," someone explained. "There'd be a special prize for second
place, I'll warrant, were he here!"

"I didn't know there was a girl entered," a man whom
Anne decided might be a judge in the race, said as he
offered his hand smilingly. "You gave the winner a real
run."

"I was driving for my cousin, Nate Crawford," Anne
explained, embarrassed at the commotion she had caused,
yet pleased by the friendly greetings, the smiles, the occasional pat on the arm. Then the winner was introduced
to her; he was shaking her hand as though it was she who
had won.

Anne searched the faces in the crowd and at last she
saw Nate. Behind him came Franklin, and suddenly Anne
felt panicked. What would Franklin think? And Nate?
Would they be as pleased as the excited, noisy men, and
the few laughing women just beyond them who had ap-
plauded her near-victory?

"Nate!" Anne called, moving from the crowd toward
her cousin. "What happened to you? Where did you go?"

Nate's eyes studied the crowd, and Anne was sure that
he was not pleased. She glanced from him to Franklin. A
puzzled expression was turning into an amused smile
as he looked from Anne to Nate's disturbed face. Finally
he laughed, as whole-heartedly as the other men who were
drifting away from the goal line.

"I guess a girl can race if she wants to, Nate," he said.
"This is a day for everyone to enjoy." Then, turning to

Anne, "A good race you ran, too. I watched you. Nobody had told me you were such a skillful horsewoman."

To Anne, it was not a compliment; a polite manner of explaining away something Susan never would have done she was sure, now that she had time to think about it. The excitement of the moment before was ebbing. Were all these people laughing at her? It hadn't seemed that way when she crossed the goal line and heard their exclamations of surprise and shouts of congratulation just a few moments ago.

"Nate could have won," she stammered. "I didn't know what to do when he wasn't there at the start. . . ."

Franklin offered his hand to help her back into the sleigh.

"You did all right," he assured her. "We'll find Susan now. She must be around here somewhere. Tell me, Miss Rogers, do you ride as well as you drive?"

Anne was glad that they caught sight of Susan then, for she was too uncomfortable to answer Franklin. Her hasty act had embarrassed Nate and made her seem like a rough, backwoods girl to Susan's brother, — a girl who didn't know what was and what was not ladylike.

If Susan was disturbed, her placid expression concealed it well. She said good bye to the friends she was with, promising to see them at the ball, and began chatting at once about arrangements for the evening. A young lady had been invited to be Nate's partner, and after supper Franklin was to go for the girl and bring her and Susan's escort back to the Williams' home so all could go to the ball together.

Anne listened to the plans, too subdued to offer more than an occasional quiet comment. This night which she had been dreaming about for so long suddenly had her cold with nervous dread. Not until she and Susan went upstairs to dress for the party was anything said about the afternoon.

"I'll fix your hair," Susan offered. "Perhaps not as nicely as Polly does it, but the best I can."

"I'm afraid it doesn't matter much how it looks," Anne said. "Not now."

"Anne, you're making too much of this," Susan said quietly. "Just stop showing how you feel and go on as you should. Then everything will be all right."

"But everyone's ashamed of me," Anne almost sobbed. "Nate and you and — Franklin."

"Let's admit it would have been better if you hadn't done it," Susan said, picking up the comb. "Even admit that Franklin was somewhat — surprised. At worst it was something you're just a little too old to have done. Now just behave as nobly for him at the ball as you did for Nate at the races and you've nothing to worry about."

Anne looked at her unhappy face in the mirror. She did indeed look worried. How could she behave nobly at the ball? She took a long breath and tried to smile.

"That's better," Susan said. "Most of the members of the Detroit Young Men's Society left the ice to trail back into town with the Governor. They didn't see you this afternoon."

Reassured, Anne dressed carefully. She would certainly mind her manners this evening.

It was a quiet and dignified Anne who finally came downstairs to meet Franklin in the living-room of his home. Carefully Susan had arranged her friend's dark hair with a cluster of curls hanging from a roll at the top of her head. The green brocade dress glistened, and around her throat Anne wore a necklace of garnets which Polly had slipped into her satchel the last minute before she left the tavern.

There was honest surprise on Franklin's face when he saw her. He bowed low and touched his lips to her gloved hand in greeting, but he offered no word of compliment. Franklin looked as proper as the Governor now, and much more striking Anne thought, with his long blond hair waving back from his dark forehead. His suit and neck-stock and ruffles all were of the same elegant style as the Governor's and his bearing was distinguished. Perhaps this gown and Polly's jewels, all in the latest style too, would help atone for her mistake, Anne thought.

She wanted to ask if Governor Mason might be at the ball, but she decided to hold her peace and wait and see. That was what everyone else at the ball seemed to be doing. Anne saw many eyes turning toward the door; heard his name on every tongue. She gained in confidence when Franklin introduced her to his friends, for the young men of Detroit looked their admiration as they bowed low before her. If anyone recognized her as the excited girl who that afternoon had raced wildly with the men across the river ice, none mentioned it.

Anne had not expected to see anyone she knew at the Mansion House but midway through a minuet she found herself looking into the face of a dark-eyed girl whom she knew she had seen before. That loosely-curled black hair and colorless skin . . . where had she seen her? Then she remembered. It was the fragile teacher who had fled from the tragedy at the settlement that first day Anne had gone to the school. She looked very different tonight. A bright red evening dress was the perfect complement to her marble complexion and raven hair.

Anne watched as she and her partner went through the steps of the dance gracefully. Not once again did the girl look at her or indicate that she ever had seen Anne. Finally Anne pointed her out to Franklin.

"I'm sure I've seen her before," she said. "Do you know her name?"

Franklin hesitated before he answered, and for a moment he looked at Anne with the questioning expression that brought back the evening when she first met him.

"Don't you know?" he asked.

"I could be wrong, but I think she's the girl who was teaching the settlement school when we first went there. Before Susan came. I only saw her for a minute or two."

"She is," Franklin said slowly. "Her name is Alice Meager and she's Dr. Brown's niece. Do you remember him?"

"Oh, yes," Anne said at once. She remembered the doctor well. "Do you know her?"

"She attended the Female Seminary here when Susan did, but they weren't great friends," Franklin explained. "I didn't know her well."

Anne had no wish to meet Alice Meager and she had no

opportunity to do so. While she and Franklin were talking there was a rustle and hasty moving about at the doorway and in another second Governor Mason was in the room. Almost immediately he came to Franklin's side and Anne knew, even before he spoke, that he had recognized her. Before all the people in the glimmering ball room the Boy Governor of Michigan acknowledged her acquaintance.

Anne bowed her head when he spoke, and curtsied ever so lightly as Polly had taught her to do. Every eye in the room was on her and her heart was beating wildly. He smiled as he stood beside Franklin, looking at her with the same appraising eye as had the other members of the Detroit Young Men's Society. He was not riding in a parade now, nor planning political strategy. He was just a friendly young man, mingling with his companions at a party, and wanting to be liked too. Anne's awe melted before his smile.

"Miss Rogers is another enthusiastic Wolverine," she heard Franklin saying. "Your great program for education has become her first love."

Anne never was able to remember exactly what the Governor said to her. Words of admiration for the nobility of her ambition they were. Then he asked an unexpected question.

"Are you teaching in one of our schools now, Miss Rogers?"

"Oh, no, Governor Mason," Anne replied. "I must go to Miss Emma Willard's School before I'm prepared to teach."

"A very good school," he said and with a polite bow he moved on to greet others who were pressing around him.

Anne breathed again. Had all gone properly? Was Franklin pleased? She waited a few moments, then looked up to find him observing her soberly.

"I didn't know you were considering Miss Willard's school," he said quietly.

"It's what Papa wants me to do," Anne replied. "Was it the right thing to say to the Governor?"

"His two sisters went there," Franklin told her. "You couldn't have made a better reply. You — well, I believe you're just the kind of girl Governor Mason thinks all young ladies of Michigan should be."

Anne wanted to question him. Just what did he mean? Was this a real compliment? She looked at him inquiringly and found his eyes smiling.

"The determination to win a race," he whispered, "the intelligence to make sensible decisions, and charming — very charming in fact — at a ball."

He smiled and extended his arm graciously. The music was starting again, and the dancing. Anne fell into step beside him, tingling with excitement. This ball was all she had dreamed it would be. Flickering lights reflected in swaying crystals on chandeliers and candelabra, ladies in beautiful gowns and gentlemen in finely tailored evening dress. Most handsome of all men in the room were the Boy Governor and her own escort. And Franklin had surely taken note of her at last.

". . . The kind of a girl Governor Mason thinks young ladies of Michigan should be . . ." The words kept coming back to her mind, and Franklin's smile and gallant manner when he said them. Did he and the Governor think alike about Michigan's young ladies? He hadn't said that, and well it might be that what he had said was but an evening's pleasantry, Anne knew. But pleasant it was to place her hand on his arm and go through the graceful steps of the quadrille with him, and he had said — indeed he had — that she was very charming at a ball!

CHAPTER

9

Bleak Spring

In the spring of 1836 new Land Offices opened in Michigan and farmers like Luther Crawford hurried to Flint and Ionia.

"Paw thinks I should go with him," Nate told Anne. "When the Land Offices at White Pigeon and Kalamazoo opened, men stood in line twenty-four hours and more, so they wouldn't lose their places. If I go along to spell him, he can get some sleep and a meal or two."

"I think someone should go with him," Anne agreed. "Either you or Oscar."

"Oscar's going all right, but he wants to get land, too," Nate said. "Paw told him he's not old enough, but he's saved every cent your Paw's paid him all winter and he's determined to try. I don't know how it'll turn out."

"Uncle Luther's sure to get a farm this spring," Anne said. "If Oscar gets one too, I wonder what we'll do at the tavern. You'll all be gone, and Polly's sick most of the time, it seems like."

—118—

Anne and Nate were in the shed where Nate was polishing the top of a black walnut stand he had made for his mother. With firm, long sweeps he rubbed wax into the surface, bringing out the fine grain of the wood.

"I made this just like the one in Polly's bedroom," he told Anne. "I made a design for a chair to go beside it, too."

He dug a scrap of paper from his pocket and handed it to Anne.

"Nate, it's beautiful!" she said. "Those back panels are like tulips. Is that what you had in mind?"

Nate rubbed harder. "I call it my tulip chair," he said. "I've another in mind that I could make out of maple wood. It would be taller and more slender and reed-like."

"Nate, you're positively a genius with wood," Anne said. "Do you know it?"

"Wood is — I don't know how to say it," Nate answered, eyes still on the stand he was polishing. "Each tree has different wood, like people have different characters. I'd make some things of one wood and other things of another wood if — "

"If what?"

"If I could only do as I want!" Nate finished impulsively.

Anne knew what he was thinking. When his father got a farm there would be no time that Nate could devote to his pleasure. The gruelling demands of the land would drain the strength out of him.

"You know what, Anne?" he asked and he lowered his voice even though there was none to hear. "You remember that day in Detroit when I didn't get back in time to enter the race?"

Only too well Anne remembered.

"I saw a man in the crowd. I'd met him at Toledo. He's a cabinetmaker from Pennsylvania and he's set up shop in Kenty County. You know what?"

"No," Anne answered eagerly. "What?"

"He's making furniture out of Michigan lumber," Nate told her. "He says he can't make it fast enough. He can sell more than he can make. He said any time I want to, I can come and work for him and he'll teach me to make fine furniture."

Nate had kept his secret to himself for months, but at last it burst out and Anne sensed the intensity of his pent-up longing.

"That's what you want to do, isn't it, Nate? That's what you should do."

He didn't answer.

"Why is it that everything's in the way of what we want to do?" Anne wailed. "I thought when you grew up, you did as you pleased. I thought only children had trouble, with grownups forever telling us what to do and keeping us from doing what we want to do. But it doesn't seem to be that way at all."

"I could do as I please," Nate replied. "Only it would hurt Paw. So tomorrow I'll have to go to the Land Office."

"And I'll have to help Aunt Ellen all day, peeling potatoes and making pies with dried apples and cinnamon stick," Anne groaned. "Polly's down with a terrible cold. And I can't teach until I've gone to Miss Willard's school and I can't go to Miss Willard's school unless Papa's business is good this year."

"You've asked him?"

"The last time he was home," Anne answered. "He wants me to go all right. Polly says it's the foremost girls' school in the country. But I can't go unless collections are good after the crops come in this fall. Papa says he's sold an awful lot on credit and used what money he could lay his hands on for buying more goods back East."

Nate wiped his perspiring forehead with the back of a wax-stained hand.

"Seems to me you could learn almost enough from Susan," he said. "You're pretty smart, Anne."

Nate was not generous with praise and Anne flushed with pleasure. But what Nate thought and what he wanted did not change the situation for either of them. Early the next morning he and Oscar left with Uncle Luther for the Land Office, and Anne did indeed work from before sun-up until late evening, for Polly was exceedingly miserable, and unable to leave her bed at all. Her cheeks were hot with fever and her whole body aching, she said.

It seemed to Anne that she had scarcely been asleep at all that night when Aunt Ellen wakened her.

"Anne, get up! Rouse yourself, girl! I need you bad."

Anne rubbed her sleepy eyes and stared at her Aunt first in amazement, then in fright. Aunt Ellen's lips were drawn tight and her face was white in the flickering light of the lamp she held in her hand. She was fully dressed and half-consciously Anne sensed that she had not been in bed at all.

"What's the matter?" Anne asked.

"It's Polly. Anne, she's real bad and you'll have to go fetch Dr. Brown. I know it's no job for a girl, in the middle of the night and cold as Greenland. But I can't save her myself. I've no more medicines."

"You mean — it's that bad?"

"She worsened in the night," Aunt Ellen said and there was no mistaking the seriousness in her voice. "She's unconscious now and I've no more quinine in the house to give her. You've got to go, and fast as you can."

Anne already was out of bed and fumbling in the half-light for her clothes.

"Bundle up warm, Anne. It's a raw night. I think you've a right to put on Nate's heavy pants and ride horseback. You can make better time."

"Where are they?" Anne asked.

"I'll fetch 'em," Aunt Ellen said as she lighted Anne's lamp. "Look in on her and see if she rouses before you go. She's never done you no wrong, Anne. She's tried every way to fix things so all would be best for you. You've no right to feel the way you do about Polly."

"I feel all right about Polly," Anne said but she knew well enough that it was not quite true.

"You've never shown it," Aunt Ellen said severely. " 'Twan't any of my business so I've said nothing. But I've felt for Polly these months past. Lost 'way out here in the wilderness, which she wa'n't used to. Working like the rest of us when she wa'n't used to that, neither. Your Paw out on the road and she worrying lest he be robbed by highwaymen, and you acting so resentful most of the time."

Then, having said what was on her mind, Aunt Ellen picked up her lamp and disappeared down the dark hall.

A lump rose in Anne's throat. It wasn't that she had not realized Polly's concern for Papa, nor appreciated her efforts on her own behalf. It was just that she hadn't been willing to admit that she, Anne, was wrong. Polly had always been thinking of what was best for Anne as well as for Papa. She had even been right about the school, and Anne realized now that she had known it ever since the trip to Detroit for the inauguration festivities. But not by a single word or act or gesture had she let Polly know that she understood. She hadn't even thanked her properly for the evening dress, or the loan of the necklace, or for playing while Susan gave the dancing lessons.

Shame and remorse came over Anne as she struggled into the clumsy underwear and woolen stockings, and pushed herself into Nate's trousers. Aunt Ellen had brought a fur-lined cap and woolen mittens, and a pistol. She stood, silently, lamp in hand, watching while Anne tied her scarf tight to hold the coat collar up around her neck.

Anne didn't say anything to Aunt Ellen, but she tip-toed into Polly's room when she finished dressing and bent over the bed. Polly did indeed appear ghastly ill. Her face was gaunt and her eyes closed, and except for her choked breathing she lay motionless.

"Hang on," Anne whispered although she knew Polly

did not hear her. "I'll be back with the doctor in no time." Then she hurried from the house.

Even the barn, with its familiar pungent smell of oats and leather and animals seemed cold and strange that night, and as Anne saddled one of the horses she chided herself for all her lack of consideration. Two hours it would take to get to the doctor's house and another two hours for him to get back to the settlement. Could Polly last that long?

Anne was glad for the snow that squeaked under her feet and for the bitter cold. On a snow-covered, frozen road the horse could go faster. A soft road, with ruts and mudholes that could throw the animal and even break a leg, would have been more dangerous, and would have slowed her down. The whiteness enabled her to see a little distance ahead too, as well as along the sides of the road.

The moon was pale and buttermilk clouds streaked the sky, blotting out the stars. Canyon-like, the white road stretched ahead, cutting the dark forest. There was nothing to be afraid of, but Anne was apprehensive, so she talked to the horse and sang snatches of songs to herself, and kept her eye out for sight of man or beast. She had the pistol. There was nothing to be afraid of. But even as she tried to reassure herself, the horse stopped abruptly. The song died in Anne's throat. Leaning over the animal's neck and straining her eyes, she saw the outline of a huge beast just a few yards ahead of them. A bear, out of hibernation early perhaps, or an elk, although she could not distinguish antlers in the darkness.

Anne reached for the pistol in her pocket but as she brought it out she knew she must not shoot in the half-dark. A wounded, enraged animal was far more dangerous than one that was merely curious.

She would shout and frighten him off. She would scream, a piercing scream. She opened her lips, but no sound at all came forth. She took two or three long breaths and patted the horse's neck. She would fire the pistol off into the air. But would that frighten the horse too? Suppose he should lunge and throw her? He was backing slowly away from the animal.

"Steady, Boy," Anne said, and having found her voice, without thought or reason she began to sing, and in rising crescendo.

"Green grow the rushes, O!"

Then she shouted it wildly, with all the force her lungs could give to the sound.

"Green grow the rushes!"

It echoed through the woods. The horse had heard Papa sing too often to be disturbed by that. The wild animal turned and went crashing through the brush, into the forest.

Anne gasped for breath.

"It must have been an elk," she said to the horse. "Come on now, get started."

She sang as loudly as she could then, until a few lights in a clearing ahead told her she had reached the end of her journey.

Anne knew where the doctor lived. She pounded on the door and waited, then pounded again. A light flickered in the window and a woman's voice, gruff with sleep or annoyance, came to her.

"Wait a minute! Just wait a minute!"

When the door opened, Anne was confronted by a distraught, middle-aged woman in heavy night clothes, lamp in hand.

"I've come for the doctor," Anne said.

"I've got sense enough to know that," the woman said crossly. "What's the trouble? Two hours' sleep he's had this night."

"It's serious or I wouldn't have come in the middle of the night," Anne replied, her voice betraying the irritation she felt at the woman's hostile attitude. "My Aunt Ellen said to tell him she's seen many cases of illness through, but she can't handle this one without help. My stepmother may die if he doesn't come."

The woman motioned her inside.

"Where do you live?" she asked a little less crossly.

"Rogers Tavern at the settlement," Anne replied. "It's Mrs. Rogers, my father's wife."

Anne realized that the woman was looking at her searchingly, and she remembered that she was wearing Nate's trousers.

"I'm Anne Rogers," she said. "I — it's an awfully cold night."

"I was a-wondering," the woman said slowly. "Be you the one that scar't the teacher out of the settlement school last spring, thinking you could get it yourself? 'Cause you didn't want to do the hard work at the tavern?"

"What?" Anne asked in astonishment.

"I heard about you," the woman went on and her tone indicated all too plainly that she did not approve of what she had heard. "That teacher you drove out lived here."

Anne had known that Alice Meager was Dr. Brown's niece. She had not known that the girl lived in the doctor's home. Her first impulse was to strike back, to defend herself. Then she thought of Polly.

"Whatever you've heard about me is of no matter now," she said sharply. "I've come for the doctor because my stepmother's unconscious. She may be dying. He's got to come."

"Sit down," the woman said, and lamp in hand she walked out of the room, leaving Anne in the darkness.

Anne pulled off her red woolen gloves and wiped her hot forehead. The accusation left her dumbfounded. She hadn't thought about how Alice Meager had explained her flight from the settlement school. Of course she had tried to justify herself in some way. What had she been saying? And to whom? To the people at the Female Seminary in Detroit?

. . . Susan? . . . Franklin? . . . Was that why he had been so concerned for his sister's welfare at the settlement, and so cool to Anne when first he met her? Susan had never mentioned the incident if she knew about it, but then, Susan would not.

Anne's worried thoughts were interrupted by the return of the light, this time in the hands of Dr. Brown. He seemed even shorter and more heavy-set than she remembered him. More bald and gray and tired looking.

"Miss Rogers?" he asked, peering at her in the lamp light.

"Yes," Anne said and stood up.

"You say your stepmother's condition is serious?"

"My Aunt Ellen said to tell you she can't pull her through alone," Anne said and there was urgency in her voice. "We have no more medicines in the house."

"I'll heat up the coffee and then we'll be off," the doctor said. "A cup will do you good."

Anne shook her head. "I'll make you a good breakfast when we get to the tavern," she promised.

"It won't take a minute to get the coffee het up," Dr. Brown assured her. "My sister, Mrs. Meager, had the fire up and the coffee hot for me when I got back tonight. And that wasn't so long ago."

"I know," Anne said and the bitterness was plain in her voice in spite of herself.

Dr. Brown looked at Anne intently for a moment. "My sister doesn't entirely approve of my doctoring," he said, "nor of my friends."

"Your friends?" Anne asked, watching as he stirred the fire into red-gold sparks with a poker.

"She says we aren't practical people, any of us," Dr. Brown went on evenly. "Reverend Pierce, for instance. Do you know him?" Then, without waiting for her reply, "He's spending the night here and we sat talking after I finally got in, when we should have been a-bed. She's right, of course."

Anne did not reply. She stared at the worn paisley spread which was draped unevenly over an unvarnished drop-leaf table. It occurred to her as the doctor talked that his sister might have told Alice Meager's story to Reverend Pierce too. It was altogether likely that she had, for certainly she seemed to be a garrulous person. And he now state superintendent of schools!

Dr. Brown handed her a cup of black coffee. There was comfort in the familiar savory odor that filled the room.

"Would you like to stay the night here and talk to Reverend Pierce in the morning," he asked poking at the fire again and not looking at Anne.

"Oh, no," Anne said quickly. "I thank you but I can't do that. Aunt Ellen's expecting me back, and Polly — " Anne's voice gave out. She had to get back to Polly. Anyway, how could she face Reverend Pierce now, not knowing what he might have heard about her?

The cup clattered against the saucer as Anne handed them back to the doctor.

"Come on then," he said and put on his coat and boots. With satchel in one hand and a warm soap stone in the other, he led the way out into the night. Anne pulled the door shut, although it stuck on the threshold and closed only after a mighty tug.

They tied Anne's horse behind the doctor's sleigh, bundled the fur lap robes close about them, and kept their feet near the warmth of the soap stone while they rode back to the settlement. It was the doctor who spoke first.

"You know, I'm surprised you didn't want to stay and see Reverend Pierce," he said at last and his voice seemed kindly. "Aren't you the girl who wanted to teach the settlement school?"

So he had heard the story too! Anne took a long breath.

"Yes, I want to be a teacher," she said, "but I know I must go to Miss Willard's school first, so why should I talk to Reverend Pierce now? Anyway, I've got to get back home tonight."

She thought she could see him nodding in the darkness, his head bent forward from his stooped shoulders.

"I'm glad, in a way, to hear you say both of those things," Dr. Brown said. "Would you like to know what Reverend Pierce said to me once? He said no man was ever born to be a statesman or a philosopher or a doctor or a teacher. They all had to be educated first."

"I know," Anne answered, trying to keep her mind on the conversation. "He talked at a Hustings at our tavern once. He didn't say just those words, but the meaning was the same."

"Another thing Reverend Pierce said," Dr. Brown went on, "is that Michigan must aim at the elevation of the character of teachers, too. He believes good teachers will make good citizens of our boys and girls, and so make Michigan a great state, and 'exalt it to empire' as he puts it."

"That's about what I heard Governor Mason say the first day I was in Michigan," Anne told the doctor. "It was because of what Governor Mason and Reverend Pierce said, that I made up my mind about teaching. But none of that matters now. Not with things as they are with Polly."

The doctor took the whip from the socket and touched it to the horses' rumps. "They're going about as fast as they can," he said. "I still say you ought to talk to Reverend Pierce, though."

"Why? Because he's heard bad reports about me?" Anne asked bitterly.

"H-m-m-m-m. I didn't say that was the reason. But since you bring it up, he may have," the doctor admitted. "You see, my sister Mrs. Meager sets great store by Alice, the teacher who started out at the settlement school. An orphan girl she is, and a niece of my sister's husband. Mrs. Meager brought her up. She sets too great store by the girl, to my way of thinking."

Anne did not reply at once. It was certain now that whatever story the white-faced teacher had told when she left the settlement, it had gone straight to the ears of the man who now was superintendent of all the schools in Michigan.

"Where is she now? The teacher, I mean," Anne asked. Perhaps she would have to see this girl Mrs. Meager had raised. It was a vague thought, half formed.

"Oh, she's all right," Dr. Brown told her. "The folks at the Female Seminary got her another school to teach, out on the road to Marshall."

Anne did not say anything more. Alice Meager had without doubt told the people who managed the Seminary that she had been driven from the settlement school. Susan had heard it, and Franklin too. It was surprising that Susan had been willing to come to the settlement at all. More surprising that Franklin had allowed it. Somehow Anne would have to compel Alice Meager to tell the truth, but right now a more serious matter crowded

Anne's own troubles out of her mind. What about Polly? What would they find when they finally got to the tavern?

Silently Anne prayed: "Dear Lord, keep Polly alive. Keep her alive for Papa and me."

The first look at Aunt Ellen's face brought relief to Anne's frightened heart. "You brought quinine?" Aunt Ellen asked as she took the doctor's coat. "I've kept cool sponges on her face and she's holding out better than I thought she could, what with being worn down by fever and ague all summer. Anne, you go to the kitchen and fetch a cup of coffee. And fix the buckwheat batter so we can get a decent breakfast for the doctor, soon as he can eat."

The kitchen clock ticked the endless minutes off as Anne waited, alone and cold with dread. She piled fresh logs on the fire and watched them smoulder, then glow into flame. Mittens, curled up in a warm corner by the hearth, sniffed and twisted in his sleep.

When the first gray mist lightened the window panes, Anne opened the kitchen door to let in the morning air. From the woodlot back of the tavern came the melodious call of the mating blue jays. Soberly Anne listened and watched the new day come in. Only once a year the blue jays sing, she remembered dully. Before spring comes in. Even if the snow lies hip-deep in the swales, the blue jays know, and she wondered how they could know, on such a morning as this, that spring would ever come.

At last Aunt Ellen came down stairs.

"The doctor thinks Polly'll be all right," she said laying a kindly hand on Anne's arm. "The crisis has passed now. I think she knows 'twas you who got the doctor. Leastways, I told her."

Anne climbed the stairs slowly. She had been trying to think of the things she would say to Polly all through the anxious hours of the night. Now she hesitated in the doorway, then stepped cautiously to the side of the bed, but no words came to her mind. Polly, eyes half closed, seemed strange and unlike herself.

"Polly," Anne whispered. "Polly — "

Polly turned ever so little and stared at Anne, then turned her face to the wall.

"Go away," she moaned.

Helplessly Anne stood by the bed, tears filling her eyes. Polly had indeed been hurt by all of Anne's resentment and ingratitude. She hadn't forgotten nor forgiven it. Perhaps she never would. And now Anne was in new trouble that she did not know how to meet, and Papa away heaven knew where at this awful time!

She heard Aunt Ellen's heavy breathing and hurrying feet on the stairs. Dr. Brown turned Anne around and pushed her gently toward the door.

"She doesn't know what she's saying," he told Anne and his tone was kind. "The crisis has passed though, and she'll live. You'd better go get some sleep."

"I was fixing the doctor some breakfast," Aunt Ellen said nervously. "Perhaps you'd best go finish it, Anne."

But Anne went to her own room and closed the door behind her. She was still dressed in Nate's heavy clothing, but she slipped between the blankets and burying her face in her own pillows she cried until she fell asleep.

10 Red Copper and Furs

Now is the time to do it, Anne," Nate said cautiously as he cleaned out the corner of the shed which had been his workshop. "I've thought about it and thought about it. If I don't do it now, I'll likely never do it."

Anne sat on the edge of a box that had served as his work bench and watched him in silence. This was a serious business.

"When Oscar didn't get a farm I knew this was the time. If I go now, Paw can take Oscar with him. Oscar wants to farm. That's how it'll work out."

"What about us at the tavern?" Anne asked. "Oscar was to stay here."

"Your Paw's got to get help anyway when we go," Nate said. "Getting one more person to take Oscar's place won't make any difference to him."

Anne twisted the ends of her bright red knitted scarf. It was late March and still cold.

"But why must you run away, Nate?" she asked. "Why can't you just explain it to Uncle Luther?"

"Because I can't, Anne," Nate said and there was agitation in his voice. "You know Paw would object. He'd never consent to it. Maw would cry or be near to it. And Oscar'd turn stubborn, like as not, thinking they didn't want him."

"But they ought to be reasonable," Anne insisted. "You've got a right to be considered too."

Nate packed the last of his small supply of tools and equipment, holding each item up to scrutinize it in the beam of sunshine that the open door let in.

"You know they won't see it my way, Anne. So what's the use talking? Words might be said that we'd regret. If I just go like this, there'll be less hard feeling. With me gone, Oscar'll be quick to go with Paw. If I talk to Paw and there's a lot of trouble, I've a feeling Oscar might take it into his head to light out."

Anne could see his reasoning.

"I'll write the letter to Paw and Maw, and after I'm well on my way you put it where they'll find it."

Anne couldn't refuse Nate but she was fearful that Papa would not approve. He was staying home now for a few days while Polly slowly got her strength back.

"I wouldn't ask you, or even tell you, if there was any better way," Nate went on. "I've thought it all out. Suppose I tried to leave the letter myself, and they found it right away and Paw started after me?"

Anne shuddered at the thought of an open clash between Nate and his father.

"Suppose I hadn't told you, and just left, and wrote after I'd got myself established in Kent County. There'd be days when Paw and Maw would be worried sick, and you and your folks, too, I guess. I don't want to hurt anyone more than need be."

"I guess your way is best," Anne finally agreed. "It'll work out just the way you plan it, that way. Oscar's the one to help Uncle Luther at the new farm, not you."

So Nate wrote the letter and gave it to Anne, and when evening came he said he was going over to Doyle's. Aunt Ellen bustled about with the late chores, and putting the twins to bed, while Uncle Luther talked long to Papa about his farm and the tools he had been overhauling, his plows and seed drills, and the new reaper a man named Cyrus McCormick down in Virginia, had brought out. He'd have Papa arrange to get one to him before crops were ready to harvest in the fall.

Anne left them talking and went upstairs. She slipped the letter onto Uncle Luther's pillow, then undressed quickly and lay on her own bed, hiding-like in the darkness, and wondering how far Nate had gone. He'd be all the way to Marshall before Uncle Luther stopped talking, she was sure.

No one suspected that Anne had any part in Nate's plans, but she admitted it honestly to her father the next day while he raked dead leaves from the tavern yard and prepared to lay out flower beds for Polly.

"I guess you couldn't do any different, Anne," Papa said when she finished her story. "You've had some hard decisions to make by yourself these last weeks, haven't you?" He leaned on his rake and looked at her earnestly as he said it.

Anne nodded but did not speak.

"I'm proud of all you've done, Anne," he went on thoughtfully. "Polly told me, and Aunt Ellen too. You were brave and unselfish that night when Polly's illness came to a crisis, and everyone gives you credit."

Anne couldn't bring herself to ask what Polly had said. More than once she had wondered whether Polly knew how she had turned away from Anne. Perhaps it was Polly now who couldn't speak of how she truly felt.

Papa leaned over to tug at a projecting root which slowly yielded its grip on the earth, to his strength.

"Now about helping Nate," he continued. "I'm always sorry when a man and his son don't see eye to eye. I'm glad that things have always been right between you and me."

Anne swallowed hard. Papa had always understood how she felt about Polly, but he'd never said a word. He knew how fond she was of Nate, too.

"Nate left in a way that would cause least grief," Papa went on. "He wrote a nice letter. Did you help him with it?"

"No," Anne answered. "He just asked me to leave the envelope where I put it, and not to do it until he'd been gone awhile. I didn't see it until this morning."

"It was a fine, understanding letter," Papa said thoughtfully. "Everything's going to turn out for the best if that

—137—

man in Kent County can be relied upon, as Nate thinks."

The Crawfords left for their farm, and Oscar with them, later that week. Papa got hired help to take their places at the tavern before he started his spring trip. Polly became sole manager of the tavern then, with no Aunt Ellen to lean upon, and gradually she began talking to Anne again more as she had done before she was taken ill. There were times, though, when they worked together without words, and there was an emptiness about the tavern, and a sense of waiting — waiting for Papa to come back.

When he returned, Anne took the first opportunity to follow him to the shed where he always arranged his stock. New stock he had now for his summer sales. Anne had heard Polly questioning him about his business and it seemed to her that Papa had not answered forthrightly. She would ask him herself, for she wanted to know.

"Papa, how is your business?" she asked. "Does it look like it's going to be good enough so I can go to Miss Willard's school by winter?"

Papa turned to look at Anne searchingly.

"Anne, tell me truthfully, is your heart still set on teaching school?"

"Yes," Anne replied. "It's more important than ever, now. You see, Papa, there's something you and I didn't know about. Something I haven't told you."

He sat down on a packing box and motioned Anne to his side.

"What is it, Anne?"

She told him then of the bitter accusation that had

confronted her the night she went to Dr. Brown's house to fetch the physician to Polly.

"And Papa," she finished, "I'm just as sure as can be that Alice Meager told that story to everyone. The people at the Female Seminary in Detroit and Reverend Pierce too. Everything the doctor said pointed that way. I've got to make that teacher tell the truth. I can't let Reverend Pierce think I just wanted to teach school so I wouldn't have to do the hard work at the tavern. He's state superintendent of schools now. — To say nothing of Susan and Franklin. Do you think they'd heard about it too?"

Papa did not betray any feeling while Anne told her story, but he put his arm around her shoulder when she finished.

"I wouldn't be surprised if they had," he said at last. "The Kirklands questioned me about it, and they talked to Susan before I saw her."

"What did Susan say?" Anne asked.

"Susan was eager to take the school," Papa assured her. "She said she remembered you well and was sure you'd be a good friend. So I didn't think any more about it. Franklin — " he hesitated, thoughtfully. "Franklin did seem pretty concerned about having Susan go so far out on the Turnpike, or so he said."

"It wasn't the distance he was concerned about," Anne said with conviction. "It was me."

He drew her closer to him, reassuringly.

"Maybe you'll have to face this girl, and in front of Mrs. Meager too," he said. "That won't be easy, but you've the right and the truth on your side. From what you tell me, you've got Dr. Brown too. You'll have to go back, on a Saturday or Sunday likely, when Miss Alice can be expected to be at Dr. Brown's."

"And after I've done that, and Reverend Pierce hears the truth of it, do you think I can go to Miss Willard's school?" Anne pressed. "I still want to be a teacher in Governor Mason's great program."

"If there's any way for me to do it, you'll go," Papa promised. "My business is growing, but not fast. The women know I never give them any wooden nutmegs, but I've had my troubles."

"Troubles? What troubles?"

"Well, that last shipment of clocks I got," he said, getting up and resuming his work at the packing boxes. "The wooden works had swollen on the trip on the canal boat and the wires got rusty. I sold them in good faith last fall, but when I made my trip over the same ground this spring, I found a lot of angry women. I've had to sit up half the night, night after night, repairing those clocks. Whittling and paring and smoothing up the works so they'd go, and I wouldn't lose customers. It's well I knew how to do it."

"Oh, Papa," Anne said sympathetically.

"Then there's the matter of how much credit to give. Little things sell all right for cash. Hooks and eyes and pins and brass buttons, But if I want to sell the silver — and that's what gives me a nice profit — I have to extend credit. I've taken in furs and grain on accounts this spring, in order to collect. I have to get enough cash to satisfy the manufacturers back East and pay the freight on the new shipments. Do you see how it is, Anne?"

"Yes, but I hadn't known," she admitted.

"Then there's the whole matter of state politics," Papa went on. "If the state goes broke, that's going to have a bad effect on my business. Both at the tavern and on the road."

"If the state goes broke?" Anne questioned. "How can a state go broke? What do you mean?"

"Our constitution actually doesn't make us a state," Papa explained. "Congress granted Federal funds for administering the old Territory, but Congress won't grant any funds for Mason's Michigan."

Anne looked her puzzlement.

"A government can't run without money, Anne," Papa explained. "Governor Mason has to have a salary in order to live. Everything costs money. The paper he writes on, the oil in the lamps, the coal to heat the capitol building, muskets and ammunition for the state militia. Everything."

"What's Governor Mason going to do?" Anne asked. He did have to get money, she could see, after Papa's explanation.

"It's hard to say," Papa told her. "Our legislature's going to tax people in some way if Congress doesn't allow us to be a state pretty soon. Michigan is losing the five percent commission on the sale of Federal lands that all states get. If Mason has to tax individual people, they'll have less money to buy my goods. It will slow up emigration to Michigan, too."

Papa wasn't the only one who was concerned about the sorry state of Michigan's affairs. Before he left on his next trip, Franklin Williams drove out from Detroit, pulling his horses to a sharp halt as they raced into the tavern yard. His face was damp and darkened with dust. Even while he was taking his tripod from his carriage, he was asking for Mr. Rogers.

"Papa's here," Anne assured him. "I thought perhaps you'd come to see Susan. She's here today," and she motioned toward the tavern. Susan had appeared in the doorway at the sound of her brother's voice and now came running to meet him.

"I was hoping to see you both, of course," Franklin said, giving his sister a quick hug. "Forgive my bad manners. But it was so important that I see Mr. Rogers that he was foremost in my mind."

The girls led him to chairs under the sheltering trees in the tavern yard and Papa came from the shed to join them. The July sun beat down through the leaves, etching a pattern in shade on the grass.

"What's the news?" Papa asked while Polly served glasses of cold fruit juice.

"The news is bad," Franklin told them. "Congress has just adjourned without taking us into the Union."

"No action at all?" Papa asked and his voice showed his concern.

"Oh, yes, there was finally some action," Franklin said. "Lucius Lyon used all his personal influence with men in the cabinet and Democrats in Congress and even with President Jackson. He finally got an Act through."

"What does it provide?" Papa asked and all waited in nervous excitement as Franklin started to explain the provisions.

"Two things, and both of them bad," he said. "First, we give up the Ohio strip and take the country north of the straits in exchange. The Upper Peninsula, Lyon is calling it. Nobody knows what we're getting, except some red copper and furs. It's a wilderness, but Lyon says we must take it. He's a surveyor and has been there. He may know more than he's saying."

"And the second provision?" Papa asked.

"The second provision is worse," Franklin said, running his fingers through his long hair nervously. "Congress won't recognize any act of ratification by our state legislature. This new Constitutional Act has to be ratified by local conventions in every county in the state. The counties have got to send their delegates to a final state convention."

Papa whistled softly.

"What does Governor Mason say about giving up the Ohio strip?" Anne asked. "Will he do it?"

"He's got to," Franklin answered. "Mason knew he'd lost the Ohio strip the day Jackson removed him from office. He'll take the Upper Peninsula if that's what Congress wants. Canada, too, if they say so. Only we've got to be a state, and now! We can't go on losing money at this rate. Michigan's lost $500,000 from the sale of Federal lands, because Congress won't turn the money over to our state government."

"It almost sounds as though Mr. Watling was right and

our action in electing Mason as governor wasn't legal,"
Anne said. "Remember the night of the Hustings, Papa,
and the day Mason was elected?"

"I do indeed," Papa admitted.

"The worst part of it all now," Franklin went on, "is
that the Whigs are doing an 'about turn' and are saying
we shouldn't give up the Ohio strip. They don't want the
Congressional Act ratified at the local county conventions
and again at the final state convention. If it is, Michigan
will get into the Union and Mason's government will be
legal. Mason'll win, if we meet the terms of Congress."

Anne put her hands to her head.

"First the Whigs say one thing and then they say the
opposite," she groaned.

"That's politics," her father told her. "They don't
want Mason to win. So whatever will defeat him, that's
what they're for."

"But they're not in the majority," Anne exclaimed.
"The majority are for Mason."

"Yes," Franklin admitted, "but here's where the trouble comes in. A lot of people who are for Mason don't
know that he's got to lose the Ohio strip in order to win
statehood. They'll vote against ratifying the Act of Congress because they think that's what Mason wants."

"How can we let them know, Franklin?" Papa asked.

"That's one of the things I came to the tavern for,"
Franklin said. "I'm on a surveying trip up into the new
counties to the north of here. I'm making it a point to
stop at every house and tell everyone I can see. The convention delegates have got to vote to ratify the Act of Con-

gress or Mason's government will fall. I was hoping I'd catch you, Mr. Rogers. You can do the same thing on the trips you make this summer."

Franklin's intensity had permeated the entire group. Papa was clasping and unclasping his hands nervously and his face was serious.

"A combination of Whigs and misinformed Democrats will ruin Mason and Michigan," Papa said thoughtfully.

"And just when he's at the height of his fame," Franklin went on. "His constitution was heralded in Washington, even by those opposing him, Lucius Lyon writes. It's militant Democracy opposed to concentrated power, he says. It's sound in every provision and far-sighted!"

He rose and paced up and down under the trees. Susan stepped to his side.

"Franklin, you take things so hard," she said. "We all want Mason to win, of course, but suppose he doesn't? Couldn't you just go on about your surveying business as you'd planned?"

"I suppose I would, Susan," he said and stopped his restless pacing. "I suppose I would, and get you back home where you belong. I'll do it before long, I promise."

"I'm all right," Susan said. "I've told you that, over and over again. I've been happy here at the settlement. It's you I'm thinking about."

Anne glanced quickly at her father. Didn't Susan's words confirm her suspicions? Probably Franklin still believed there was truth in Alice Meager's story, but surely he must know that Susan was loved and well cared for in the Rogers home, and in the entire community.

Foremost in Franklin's mind now were Mason and the future of Michigan, his next words revealed. He patted Susan's arm by way of answer and turned to Papa again.

"The Whigs control most of the small country newspapers, Mr. Rogers," he said. "Did you know that? The convention's going to be held in Ann Arbor on September 26th. A handful of us can scarcely cover the state before then and give the people the true facts. They'll believe what they read in the papers. I'm frightened to death for Mason and Michigan."

"We all have cause to be," Papa agreed. "I'm worried about my business, and Anne's plans to go to Miss Willard's school, but we'll do what we can out here, Franklin. You can tell Governor Mason he can depend on that."

Throughout the summer the Whigs held meetings in county courthouses and town halls. In their country newspapers, they agitated against bowing to Governor Lucas and losing the Ohio strip. At every grist mill and saw mill and tannery, the old Whig office-holders harangued the backwoods farmers. The sheriff, the clerk, the register, the treasurer, the judge, the coroner, the surveyor — they were important men. Many had held office since the township lines were set, back in 1825 when Congress gave authority to the Territory to organize county governments. So the voters chose these men, or others they selected, as delegates to the Ann Arbor convention, and there they voted, by twenty-eight to twenty-one, to reject the Act of the United States Congress which would have made Michigan a state.

Thus Governor Mason lost.

Franklin hurried to the tavern with the news.

"Is your father home?" he asked Anne almost before he was out of his carriage.

"No, Franklin, but do stay the night," Anne said. "We expect him any day now. Tomorrow, perhaps. Susan will want to see you too."

Franklin unhitched his tired horses and picketed them to graze. He was so obviously distressed by the turn of events that he was not thinking about either Anne or his sister, and there was little Anne could say to interest him.

"Where's Susan boarding this week?" he asked. "If it isn't far, let's walk over and get her. I'm in no mood to sit quietly and visit, I'm afraid."

Taking a short cut through the woods, they set off together in the late afternoon sunshine to the home of a neighbor where Susan was spending the week. Mostly they walked in silence, Anne hurrying to keep up with Franklin's long, rhythmic strides. Pewees and robins sang, and the small noises of forest insects shrilled against the quietness of the day. Anne would have chosen to stroll more leisurely, and enjoy the beauty the first frost had brought to the trees but Franklin was in no such happy mood. He scarcely asked how she and Susan had fared since he saw them last, and Anne knew there was nothing to talk about except Mason. Some day she must tell Franklin just what had happened at the school house the day she first saw Alice Meager. This walk, alone with him through the wood-lot, with the fallen leaves rustling crisply beneath their feet, should have been the time. Clearly it was not.

"What is this action by the county delegates going to do to Governor Mason?" Anne finally asked.

"It's going to ruin him if something isn't done," Franklin told her. "That's why I must see your father. There's a plan afoot. It might work."

"What is it?" Anne asked.

Franklin shook his head and his lips pressed into a severe, thin line.

"I'd rather not talk about it, Anne," he said. "Not until I've seen your father, at least. But this I can tell you. If something isn't done, Mason and our whole state government are ruined. Our legislature will have to disband and Mason will have to resign. I don't know what the Whigs have got up their sleeves, but they have their own plan for getting Michigan into the Union, after they've ousted Mason."

"Franklin, that can't be," Anne almost cried. "He's the greatest man in Michigan."

"He's one of the most promising men in the whole country," Franklin replied. "Perhaps the people can save him yet. He's still their idol."

"Those delegates didn't sense what they were doing at Ann Arbor," Anne wailed.

"Some of them know it now," Franklin replied bitterly. "Well, as I said, there's a plan afoot."

Anne and Susan and Polly had to content themselves with that little grain of information while Franklin waited for Papa. Evening came, and they brightened a bit when Polly played her melodeon and they all sang. Later, sitting on the stoop, Susan slipped her arm through Franklin's and linked her fingers into his. A little lonely, Anne sat apart; and in silence they watched the great, golden moon rise. Someday Franklin would take Susan home to Detroit and her friends in the gay capital city, and that special friend who still wrote regularly from New York. She would surely miss them both when that day came. It well might mean that she would see no more of Franklin. Not once since the night of the ball had he shown more than a polite friendship for Anne, yet not to see him again was as bad to think about as the defeat of Governor Mason.

The next day Papa came home and he and Franklin at once went to the shed.

"I know there's no use questioning them, but I do wish they'd tell me what's afoot," Anne said to Polly while they worked together in the tavern kitchen.

"We might not like it altogether if we knew," Polly answered. "I'm fearful it's some scheme that will take your father from his business, just like Franklin is neglecting his. Now is the time your father should be making his collections. Farmers have money this time of year."

Anne did not answer. It was important that Papa should make his collections, of course, but it was also important that Governor Mason should somehow be kept in office. That affected Papa's business, too, as he had explained to her earlier in the summer. Somehow neither Polly nor Susan seemed to fully realize that.

It was soon clear that the men did not intend to talk about their plans. Franklin avoided Anne's eyes when he said good bye in the morning, but he told her he'd stop at the tavern again soon.

"Try to stop on your way back," Anne said, hoping the invitation sounded polite and that her eagerness to see him again had not crept into her voice. She stroked the shining flank of one of his carriage horses as she spoke.

Franklin hesitated beside her and for a moment the tenseness left his face.

"It won't be that soon," he said slowly. "This trip has to be made in a circuit. But after the campaign is over. . . ."

He left the sentence unfinished and looked beyond Anne to the beckoning road.

"Remember the night in Detroit when we all went to the inaugural ball?" he asked. "There'll be evenings like that again. I've promised Susan, and you'll be there too. Now I've a task to finish, but after that, well, I keep hearing the call of the Turnpike with you and Susan both out here. I'll be back."

He smiled as he jumped into his carriage and waved to her as he drove out of the yard, leaving those words with Anne to be remembered and dreamed about.

Papa spent two days with the men at the settlement, visiting first one then another. It was little enough that either Anne or Polly saw of him, and Anne had so much that she wanted to ask and say. For one thing, she had made two fruitless visits to the home of Dr. Brown. Neither time had Alice Meager been there. Nor would Mrs. Meager tell her when she might be. So what was Anne to do now? Alice was teaching near Marshall and Anne could go to her school, but if anything was to be settled, it must be settled with Mrs. Meager too, Anne was sure.

Polly also watched for Papa's return each day, and it was she who finally questioned him about the nature of the work he was doing.

"I've been wondering, Mr. Rogers, how much time this plan of Franklin's is going to take," she said as they sat together at the dinner table.

"Time?" Papa repeated. "Why, what do you mean?"

"Right now is the time when collections can be made," Polly reminded him. "You've said you were extending credit to too many of your customers, perhaps. I just wondered if this business Franklin proposed isn't working to your own disadvantage."

Papa tilted his chair back and smiled across the table, and it was good to Anne to see his face lighten.

"What a woman for business you're getting to be," he said. "Reminding your husband he must still be the provider! Well, I'll start in the morning and make collections at every stop, I promise you. Don't you worry your pretty head about this plan of Franklin's, or the collections either. I'll bring the money home this trip, and make no mistake."

The following day he was off, but Anne realized when he drove out of the yard that he was not singing.

Papa was still quiet when he returned, and he prepared to set out again with little or no rest between trips. Indian summer had faded now and the chill of winter was in the air, so he brought out the fur lap robes and the soap stones. Before he left he had a few words alone with Anne.

"I want to leave a message with you for Franklin, in case he should come to the tavern before I return," he said. "Tell him I met with good success on the trip east along the Turnpike. Tell him I have Governor Mason's edict, and that I'm taking it with me as I work west now. He'll know what I mean."

"I wish I knew," Anne said.

"Isn't it enough to know that I'm working for Governor Mason?" her father asked. "I've been doing good business at the same time, Anne. I must tell Polly that cash collections were better than ever this fall. Crops are sold and our Michigan wheat shipped back East. The farmers have money and things may all turn out right. For you as well as Governor Mason."

Anne brightened, but the load did not quite lift from her heart. Papa still wasn't singing when he drove away, and it had been a long time since she had seen his carefree, teasing gestures.

It started snowing that morning, and by night the trees were slung with white, and the road and clearing heavily carpeted. Anne piled logs on the fires to keep the tavern cheerful while the wind whined and howled outside. There were few guests, and those who had stopped for the night went to bed early.

Anne was alone in the kitchen when she heard the sound of horses' hooves in the yard, and the scraping of a wagon against the side of the building. Her first thought was of Franklin, but he knew the tavern yard too well to miss the driveway and crowd his rig against the house. Puzzled, she stood listening, but no sound of voices nor of people alighting, came to her. Then as she waited the high, wavering neigh of a horse startled and chilled her.

Anne ran to the kitchen door and pulled at the bolt, her hands clumsy with fear. Behind her came Polly's hurrying steps. She, too, must have heard the cry of the horse.

Then in the cold white light of the high November moon, Anne stared aghast at her father's own team and his driverless peddler's wagon.

"Polly!" Anne called in horror. "Polly!"

The animals were pawing the snow and tossing their heads. Anne and Polly ran to the wagon, searching in the dimness, feeling through the merchandise, peering beneath the wagon.

"Papa," Anne called over and over, her voice scarce above a whisper. "Papa!"

There was no answer.

"Get a candle, Anne," Polly said hoarsely. "Or better, the lantern. In this wind a candle's not safe."

But the light revealed nothing.

"I'll take the team and start back along the road," Anne said, starting to the house for her coat. "I can follow the tracks in the snow."

"No," Polly said as she followed Anne. "We'll take the sleigh Nate left and a fresh team. We can make faster time. I'll rouse the hired man and have him put these horses up."

"But I can't wait," Anne protested. "He's hurt. He's been thrown out and hurt. He's lying somewhere. . . ."

"Anne, don't lose your head," Polly said sharply. "What are you going to do, all alone, if you find him injured? A broken leg and not able to stand, perhaps. You're not going alone. We've got to get Mr. Doyle or the sheriff or both. Now do as I say."

Polly was right, and Anne was too frightened to take offense at her unexpected sharpness. She ran for her fur-lined coat, pulled her heaviest red wool stocking cap over her head, and took the mittens Polly handed her. Before she had the team hitched to Nate's sleigh, Polly joined her. She had shoved all her clustering curls up under one of Papa's fur caps and was tieing his gray knitted scarf around her neck. Even in the moonlight she looked strange, and older somehow, in this attire.

At Mr. Doyle's they waited nervously while he got into boots and coat. Too much time was being lost, but Anne could do nothing about it. Mr. Doyle insisted they must tell the sheriff too, which meant another stop and more time spent in repeating the story. The sheriff agreed to follow with his own team, so at last they left the settlement behind and were out on the empty Turnpike.

The wind had blown fresh snow across the road but the tracks were discernible in the clear moonlight. Mr. Doyle leaned over one side of the sleigh, Polly the other searching the road ahead and the clearings at the side for traces of an accident, while Anne, crowded between them, looked first to one side then the other.

"If he was just thrown out of the rig some way, he may be a-walking home," Mr. Doyle suggested reassuringly.

"No, Mr. Doyle," Polly said quietly. "He'd have borrowed a horse somewhere and we'd have met him before now."

Anne knew that Polly was right, and so did Mr. Doyle.

He said no more and they drove without talking for mile after lonely mile. Suddenly Mr. Doyle reached for Anne's hand and gripped it firmly.

"Steady, Anne," he said as he pulled the horses to a halt. "Steady, girl. Let me do this."

But Anne paid no heed to him. Rising in the sleigh and peering ahead she could see the patch of black beside the road that had caught his eye, and the rippling drifts of loose snow blown against it.

She heard Mr. Doyle repeating the words, "Let me do this," but she followed him out of the sleigh, Polly close behind her.

Mr. Doyle bent over and felt of her father's hands and head, then kneeling in the snow he crossed himself.

"We'll take him to Dr. Brown's," he said as he rose to his feet. "Lord bless us and save us. The sheriff's right behind. You two go back to the sleigh."

Neither Polly nor Anne moved, nor did Mr. Doyle. Speechless they stood in the snow, watching cloud shadows pass over the darker shadow at their feet. Slowly Anne realized that her father was dead. That it made no difference whether they went to Dr. Brown's or not. This white stillness . . . this unearthly night . . . how could this strangeness be real? Papa had left her in the morning, quiet and not singing. She would never hear him sing again. That was the only thought that came to her clearly.

Not until the sheriff came did Anne and Polly return to Nate's sleigh.

"There's nothing you can do now," the officer said to

Polly. "Ride on with Doyle to Dr. Brown's. I'll be following right behind."

When Polly did not answer, he took her by the shoulders and turned her around. She stumbled in the snow as he half-pushed her back to the sleigh and Anne, groping beside her, reached out a hand lest she should fall but Polly seemed not to see her. Then the clip-clop of the horses' hooves, the creaking of runners on frozen snow, as they drove to the doctor's home, Polly staring blankly at the dull whiteness that covered road and clearing and forest, silent and stunned.

Still silent they waited with Mr. Doyle in the doctor's parlor, huddled near the fire, listening to the wall clock as it loudly ticked away the futile seconds. Anne's eyes were fixed on the sagging leaf of the old walnut table. Dimly she remembered it, and wondered what had become of the paisley spread. At last the sheriff came out of the examining room, Dr. Brown behind him.

"Too many people knew he carried money," the sheriff said, looking away from Anne and Polly. "He was hit over the head with a sand bag. From behind. Them tracks in the snow. Mebbee you didn't take no notice of them."

Anne had not looked at the tracks. What was he saying? "Too many people knew he carried money." Subconsciously she remembered other words. . . . "I'll bring the money home this trip, and no mistake."

"It was clear where another rig had pulled up along side," the sheriff was saying. "Then they turned around and started back the way they come from. I'll try to follow them tracks now. His money bags is gone, but his political papers was still in his pocket."

The sheriff had the papers in his hand.

Dr. Brown, who had been standing in the background, walked to Polly's side and placed his hand lightly on her shoulder.

"I don't think he ever knew what happened," he said softly. "He just thought another rig was passing. There wasn't any sign of a struggle."

Polly only shook her head and stared at the fire.

Anne turned to the sheriff who hesitated in the doorway. She tried to speak but a choking sob came instead. She held out her hand and the sheriff gave her father's papers to her.

CHAPTER 12

The Mission for Mason

Doubled over the high seat of the peddler's wagon, away in the back of the shed, Anne cried out her grief. Polly let her alone and so did Aunt Ellen and Nate, who had come as soon as word of Papa's death reached them. Only Nate ever knew of the bitterness that tortured Anne; only Nate ever saw her cry.

"It needn't have been," she sobbed when he came upon her quite by accident as he stumbled in the half-light of the shed for a tool he wanted. "It shouldn't have happened."

"What do you mean, Anne?" he asked, climbing to the driver's seat and moving her over gently, to sit beside her.

"The money. He was killed for the money," Anne sobbed. "She was urging him all the time lately to make his collections. About the last thing I ever heard him say was that he must tell Polly collections were good."

"But Anne, you can't blame her for that," Nate reasoned. "He'd have made his collections if she'd never mentioned it. Highwaymen looking for travelers with money likely had him spotted long ago. Why, they'd have done it just the same if he hadn't collected a cent, provided they thought he had. Certainly you're not blaming Polly!"

Nate put a hand timidly on Anne's arm when she did not reply.

"Anne, you've got to get that out of your mind," he told her. "It's wrong. Look at her now. Hollow-eyed as though she hadn't slept in weeks."

"I've never seen her cry," Anne said, quieting her own sobs and drying her eyes.

"Likely she hasn't seen you, either," Nate suggested. "You've got to be fair, Anne. You're building up something that would hurt your Paw mightily, if he knew it. All you've got to do is look at Polly to see how it is with her. She doesn't even look the same. No color or anything. Don't make things worse by holding such ideas as this."

Anne stuffed her handkerchief in her pocket.

"Another thing, Anne," Nate went on. "The night it happened the sheriff gave you some papers. What did you do with them?"

"I've got them. Why?" Anne asked.

"Don't you think you should let the rest of the family know what they are?" Nate asked. "Polly knows you took them. She told Maw. But she won't ask you what they were and Maw doesn't want to. Don't you think others have a right to know what the papers were?"

Anne stared down at the wagon wheels and did not answer at once.

"I was going to tell them," she said after a moment's silence. "There's something I've got to do about them."

"Then get the papers and tell us about it now," Nate said. "Come on."

Nate waited with his mother and Polly while Anne went to her own room. She knew he would be telling them something of what had passed between them, so she offered no explanation when she came downstairs, but handed the first sheet of paper directly to Nate. He glanced at it, then looked at Anne.

"It's signed 'Mason'," he said, almost in awe.

"Read it. Aloud," Anne said.

" 'If you are dissatisfied with the decision of the September convention, the remedy is with yourselves,' " Nate read. " 'You have the inherent and indefeasible right in all cases or propositions coming before you in your original capacity, to reverse the acts of your agents if found to be prejudicial to your interests.' And it's signed 'Mason'." Nate concluded.

"The rest of these sheets are lists of names," Anne said, laying the papers on the table. "You can see. There are county names. Hillsdale, Cass, Branch, Berrien, Calhoun. With each county there are names of people and the addresses or something that tells where they live."

"Is that all?" Nate asked, picking up the papers hesitantly.

"Not quite," Anne answered. "Opposite some of the names you'll find a 'y' and beside one or two there's an 'n'. Most of the letters seem to be in Papa's handwriting, but I'm not sure all are."

"Now what would that mean?" Aunt Ellen asked. Polly, meantime, sat quietly in her chair, saying nothing at all.

"It's clear enough to me," Anne said. "Papa was asking these men to do something for Governor Mason. Some were saying they would, but a few were saying 'no'. What I've got to do is find out what he was asking of them, so I can finish the list."

Aunt Ellen raised a restraining hand.

"Anne, girl, it's a noble purpose you have in mind. He had no son to complete his work, 'tis true. But it's not fitting that a girl should be taking part in politics."

"This is different from politics I'm thinking, Aunt Ellen," Anne said. "Papa was no one to be taking part in politics. This was something of great importance to our state, I know. He left a message with me for Franklin and it's tied up with this. I wish Franklin were here."

"Didn't Susan send word to Franklin?" Nate asked.

"She did, but we've had no message back. Susan thinks he's out in the backwoods counties somewhere doing the same work Papa was engaged in."

"But Anne," Aunt Ellen continued, "You've got to give up this idea of doing the thing your Paw and Franklin were doing. Stay here, peaceful like, until Polly hears from her brother Eb. Then come to us. You've got a home with us and welcome, Anne. Both of you, if Eb doesn't soften his heart toward Polly."

Aunt Ellen's insistence brought Anne almost to the point of tears again.

"Aunt Ellen, don't you see?" she pleaded. "I'm grateful to you. Where else could I turn but to you? But this means life or death to Mason. It was the last thing. . . ."

Anne thought she could not finish the sentence, but she took a deep breath and went on, waving aside her aunt's objections.

"Likely I can never take my place in the Governor's plan for Michigan now," she said. "There's no way for me to go to Miss Willard's school. Maybe all I'll ever be able to do is finish Papa's work."

"But Anne," Aunt Ellen sighed and turned appealingly to Polly.

"Sister Ellen, can't you see it's in the girl's heart and soul?" Polly asked, staring into the fire that was smouldering low, and not looking at Anne. "It's not in me to say 'no' to her now. Not if she can see clearly what's to be done and a sensible way to do it."

Anne was surprised at Polly's words. Surprised and shamed, too, and she did not look at Nate or Aunt Ellen. Aunt Ellen had always favored Polly, but now Polly was taking sides with Anne and against Aunt Ellen. Anne was glad that only Nate knew what thoughts she had been harboring. Nate would never tell.

Aunt Ellen took the poker and turned the half-burned logs.

"You were always like a son to him, 'tis true, Anne," she said resignedly. "Do as you will. And when Polly hears from her brother, you come to us."

It was all too clear that in Aunt Ellen's mind there was only one way. Polly would go back East to her brother

Eb, and Anne would live with Aunt Ellen and Uncle Luther.

"Anne, I'll wager Mr. Doyle will know what mission your Paw was on," Nate suggested after a few minutes. "Like as not he talked to Mr. Doyle, first off. If Franklin doesn't come tomorrow before I go back to Kent County, I'll go with you to Mr. Doyle and we'll see what's to be done."

"You must go tomorrow?" Anne asked. She would have had him stay longer, for his slow, sure ways were comforting.

"I'm expected back, Anne," he replied. "I'll have to go."

But Franklin came that night. Tired-eyed he was, with a stubble of corn-colored beard covering his cheeks and chin. Never before had Anne seen him when he was unkempt and not shaven.

"Franklin!" she exclaimed in answer to his knock. "You are ill? What's wrong?"

His hand shook as he set his tripod against the wall. "Nothing but lack of sleep," he said. "I've been driving day and night for weeks. I came just as soon as I got back to Detroit and found the message."

His arm across her shoulders was comforting. He walked beside her to the sofa and together they sat down.

"No words can help you, Anne," he said gently, "but you have a memory that is given to few, for few men are as fine and honorable as I came to know your father to be."

Anne could not answer. She was glad when Aunt Ellen

came bustling from the kitchen bringing hot cider and cinnamon stick. Polly already had gone to her room.

"I'm glad you came, Franklin, though it was hard on you," Anne said at last. "Papa left a message for you and I have his papers. Now I must know the nature of the work he was doing."

"What message, Anne?" Franklin asked, overlooking her last words.

"He said to tell you he had good success on the trip east along the Turnpike and that he was taking Governor Mason's edict on the trip west. I have it, and the list of names. All the 'y's' mean yes and the 'n's' mean no, don't they?"

Franklin nodded and went over the names, counting carefully.

"He did good work," he said. "Now it's up to me to carry on."

"No, Franklin," Anne said, reaching for the list. "You had your own assignment. I'll finish my father's task. Just you tell me what it was he was doing."

Franklin stared at Anne, apparently disbelieving his ears.

"You?" he asked. "Anne, child, you're brave I know, but this is no job for a girl."

"Tell me the plan," Anne urged.

For a few moments Franklin watched the blazing logs. He rested his head in his hands as he bent near the warmth of the blaze.

"Perhaps she could help," he said at last. "Nate, what do you think?"

"I could answer better if I knew what Uncle Mart was about," Nate replied. "You forget, Franklin, that we don't know. To us it's a mystery."

"That's right," Franklin apologized. "I forgot for the moment that you weren't a part of the movement, Nate. It had to be kept quiet at first." Then he drew a long breath and began.

"The plan's simple as can be," he said slowly. "We're calling another convention to reverse the action taken in September. We've set about getting delegates from every county to go down to Ann Arbor again. The date set is December fourteenth. There must be seventy delegates present. That's way beyond the number present in September. Then they must make the action unanimous and in favor of the Act of Congress that would admit us to the Union. It was a narrow vote that defeated Mason in September and kept us out. This vote has got to be conclusive."

Nate and Anne listened attentively, almost afraid to breathe lest they miss a word.

"A small group of us—committeemen we're calling ourselves—have been going to every county in Michigan," Franklin went on. "We've shown the loyal Democrats the statement Anne has here, and we've told them what's to be done. It's imperative. Otherwise our state government's gone, our constitution's gone, and the Whigs will have beaten Mason. He'll have to resign."

Anne nodded as the plan became clear to her.

"These are the men to see?" she asked, pointing to the list.

"Yes," Franklin said, peering at the names over her shoulder. "Do you know any of them?"

"Dr. Brown," Anne replied. "I've heard of one or two others."

"Then start with Dr. Brown," Franklin told her. "Suppose you take Branch County. I'll go west to Lake Michigan and work back. And Anne, if Dr. Brown should offer to help you, let him do it. Don't be stubborn."

"I wouldn't be stubborn," Anne said.

"You might," Franklin admonished. "It's too important to Mason for you to refuse help. I'm not belittling your ability, Anne, nor the earnestness of your purpose. I've come to regard them both highly. But in a matter of such grave importance, men scarcely expect a girl to be carrying the message. Only the circumstances—"

"Franklin's right, Anne," Nate interrupted. "It's a man's job, and if Dr. Brown or some other man you can trust offers to carry on, then you mustn't stand in the way of it. Much as you want to do the job yourself. A girl, refusing men's help, could hurt Mason's cause. You must see that, Anne. You could be misunderstood."

Franklin and Nate were both looking at her intently. Anne hoped the flickering light from the burning logs would hide the flush that came to her cheeks. But she understood their caution. They were right. She had been misunderstood before as they both knew.

"I'll go to Dr. Brown first," she promised. "He knows me. I'll be guided by him in making the next move."

"Then you take these names," Franklin said and divided the list, keeping the greater part for himself.

Anne did not argue. She took the list he gave her and put it away carefully in the highboy. Nate and Franklin both were skeptical, she was sure, but they didn't mistrust her altogether. She would prove to them both that she could carry on, as Papa would have wanted her to do.

CHAPTER 13

Tasks Completed

Anne was prepared for an unfriendly greeting from Mrs. Meager when she knocked at the doctor's door. She was not prepared for the sight of Alice Meager. Thin faced as Anne remembered her, black curling hair in a loose knot on the top of her head, she was attractive even in the faded blue wrapper she was wearing. For a moment they both stood, silenced by surprise, at the doorway. Then Anne's wits came back to her.

"Is Mrs. Meager home?" she asked.

Alice Meager swallowed before she stepped aside for Anne to enter. She mumbled "Come in" then called nervously, "Aunt Moll! Oh, Aunt Moll!"

Anne tugged at the door and pulled it shut behind her. It always seemed to stick and sag on its hinges. And the sagging table leaf. That hadn't been replaced either. Perhaps this was why Mrs. Meager didn't entirely approve of her brother's doctoring, as Dr. Brown himself had told her the second time she saw him. Anne glanced about the room and waited for Mrs. Meager to come. There was a slat missing from one of the ladder-back chairs too, and the hand-braided rug was threadbare. She hadn't noticed it before.

A curt, "How-de-do," ended Anne's appraisal of the Doctor's scantily furnished parlor. "Who's took now?" Mrs. Meager demanded. She did not sit down or offer Anne a chair.

"Nobody," Anne replied. "I came to see the Doctor on business, but I'm glad for a chance to see you both at last," and she glanced at Alice who had picked up a lamp chimney from the table where she apparently had set it down when she answered Anne's knock. She began drying it clumsily.

"You come to see the Doctor on business?" Mrs. Meager asked tartly. "What kind of business? School business?"

"Yes," Anne replied with equal sharpness. "School business. And you and Miss Alice, too."

Alice turned her back to Anne and replaced the chimney on a small wall lamp. It wasn't shining as Aunt Ellen had taught Anne to polish lamp chimneys but it was clean.

"I've been trying for months to see you both, as you know," Anne continued before Mrs. Meager could speak again. "I want to hear exactly what Miss Alice said happened the first day I went to see about starting to school at the settlement."

Both Mrs. Meager and Anne looked at Alice, who stood fumbling with the wall lamp.

"You went to see about starting at school?" Mrs. Meager repeated. "You mean you was going to attend school? To study?"

A puzzled look came over Mrs. Meager's face. She and Alice even looked alike, Anne thought, only Mrs. Meager was so much more positive, her expression so set and determined.

"That's what I went to school for that first day," Anne said. "I told Miss Alice that I was likely going to attend school, and my cousins, too, if Papa settled in the neighborhood as he was considering."

Mrs. Meager looked quickly at Alice. "Is that right?" she asked.

"I don't recall exactly what she said," Alice replied. "She might have said it." She looked at Mrs. Meager for a second, then at the dish towel in her hand and she did not once look at Anne.

"What do you recall?" Anne demanded. "That's what I want to know. I want to know what you told Mrs. Meager and Reverend Pierce. I've got a right to know."

Alice cleared her throat.

"Well . . . m-m-m-m- I just told Aunt Moll what happened, that's all."

"That's what I want to hear," Anne insisted. "I want to hear what you said happened."

Alice "m-m-m-'ed" again. "I can't recall exactly what was said now," she hedged. "I just told what happened."

"Look, Mrs. Meager," Anne said turning to the older woman. "Don't you think in fairness I've a right to know what's been said? If it's the truth, I've no quarrel with it."

—171—

Mrs. Meager hesitated and looked at Alice dubiously. "She has a right, Alice," she said at last.

"Well, all I said was how she come to the school," Alice began. "Then she called me out and . . ."

"And what?" Anne pressed, but there was no answer.

Mrs. Meager, who had been standing, motioned Anne to a chair while she herself sat down heavily on an old horse-hair sofa.

"Mebbee you'd best tell me your side of it, Miss Rogers," she said. " 'Tis true I've only heard the one side, and that's the side I myself told Reverend Pierce. Alice didn't tell him. I did. I ask't him to tell the folks at the Female Seminary too, so she could get another school. That was before he was state superintendent."

So Anne told Mrs. Meager of the child who had fallen into the unguarded well at the school house and of everything that had happened, just as she remembered it. As she talked she had a feeling of confidence; confidence that Mrs. Meager would be fair.

"Mrs. Meager, I hadn't an idea in the world of teaching that school when I went there. Not until Mr. Doyle asked me," Anne said as she finished her story. "And that was after Miss Alice had packed her satchel and started for home. After he asked me, I admit I wanted to do it. But when I told Papa and his wife, they both said I couldn't until I'd gone to school longer myself. So I never had a chance to teach that school."

Mrs. Meager wiped her hands on her hips as Anne finished talking.

"What have you got to say, Alice?" she asked, her chin jutting forward a little.

"Well, that's about as I said," Alice replied. "Only she didn't say how she glared at me and frightened me 'till I was out of my wits and didn't know what I was doing. She made out like I'd been the one who . . . was responsible for the . . . drowning," and she whispered the word as though it still frightened her.

Anne was on her feet instantly.

"That's not true!" Anne insisted, her fingers tightening over the back of her chair. "I never once thought of blaming you. Mr. Doyle didn't say you were to blame. Nobody did."

"I didn't say Mr. Doyle said it," Alice mumbled.

Mrs. Meager was nodding and making little clucking noises.

"The one who thought you was to blame was you yourself, Alice," she said. "You were scar't all right. And mebbee you did scare her," she said turning to Anne. "But I see what's at the bottom of it now."

"Then you believe me?" Anne asked.

"I believe you. And her, too. Your stories aren't too different. It's just that Alice has been blaming herself all the time for the accident, and scar't others was blaming her too, and trying to protect herself by throwing the scent off on someone else."

At Mrs. Meager's words, Alice settled slowly into a chair, and turning sidewise, hid her face against the back of it. The dejected, sagging shoulders were a sorry sight, but while Anne was wondering what to do or say there was the sound of a scraping door and Dr. Brown came out of his examining room. Mrs. Meager nodded in his direction without looking at him.

"You said you come to see the Doctor on business," she said. "There he is."

Dr. Brown motioned to Anne. "Come in," he said.

It was the first time Anne had ever been in the Doctor's examining room. There was a worn horse-hair couch against one wall and above it hung the Doctor's framed diploma. Two china cabinets, filled with medicines and instruments, extended along one wall and books filled the other. Dr. Brown nodded toward one of two straight-backed chairs. When he tilted back on the other, Anne saw that the rungs were loose, and once more thought that perhaps Mrs. Meager had some reason for wishing he would pay attention to something beside his doctoring and his friends.

Dr. Brown lit his pipe and settled back comfortably.

"I heard it all," he said without any pretense of apology. "It's about as I thought. You need have no fear about Moll correcting any false impression she gave Reverend Pierce. She's a fair woman, is Moll."

He drew in on his pipe and puffed the aromatic smoke out slowly.

"What was it you came to see me about?"

It was a relief to talk about the plan which Papa and Franklin had been working on, and the unfinished list of names the sheriff had given her. She could talk freely and earnestly about the task to which she had set herself, now that the matter of the settlement school and Alice Meager was cleaned up. Not that it mattered much any more. Not to anyone but herself.

The Doctor listened, nodding now and then.

"Let me see the list," he said. The list seemed more important to him than Governor Mason's edict. Anne gave the papers to him.

"Do you know these men?" she asked.

"All of them," he assured her. "You're planning to see them? To tell them?"

"They're the ones on my father's list," Anne replied. "They must be seen. Or others, if you have better names to propose."

"No better names," he said. "I'm going down the Turnpike on the next call. If you'd like, I'll take you along and introduce you. Sort of get you started."

"I'd be indebted to you," Anne told him. It was not necessary for her to remind herself of Franklin's warning. It was indeed a relief to have the Doctor offer to go with her.

Tinkling bells hung from the neck-yokes of the Doctor's horses, their cheerful notes ringing clear in the winter air. There was a quiet assurance about this short, pouchy man that Anne always sensed when she was with him. It put her at ease now.

"When people hear those bells they'll know it's me arriving, once they get used to the idea," he told Anne. "I just thought of it the other day."

"It's a wonderful idea," Anne told him. "I'm glad you thought of it."

"Have you any ideas for yourself yet?" the Doctor asked. "Seems to me I recall your telling me that you hoped to go to Miss Willard's school. Is that going to be possible now?"

Miss Willard's School! The thought made Anne heartsick. There wasn't any possible way for her to go now. She bit her lip and shook her head, and did not otherwise reply to the Doctor.

"What are you going to do?" he asked after studying the snowy clearing for a moment.

"My Aunt Ellen's offered me a home with her," she told the Doctor. "Polly too, in case she doesn't go back East to her brother Eb."

"I was just getting around to ask about Polly," he said. "Going back East, eh? Well, maybe that's best for her. I couldn't say. But a farm up Ionia-way. Is that the thing for you?"

Again Anne shook her head.

"I don't know what else," she said. "I keep trying to think. If Polly weren't to go to her brother . . . Well, I don't know."

"Maybe something could be worked out," the Doctor said thoughtfully. "Anyway, here we are, at Oakley Bean's tannery."

Oakley Bean was rightly named, Anne decided as she looked at him, trying not to be frightened. Tough as an oak he was and thin as a bean pod, and with every other tooth missing. His chin was sharp and his cheeks sunken, and the knuckles of his huge hands were large and wrinkled. When Dr. Brown introduced Anne he nodded indifferently, planted a foot on the step of the sleigh, and turned back to the Doctor.

"Well, Doc, what's on yer mind?" he asked.

"Something pretty serious," Dr. Brown replied. "Miss Rogers' father was engaged in important work for the State of Michigan when — well, perhaps you heard about it."

Oakley Bean nodded.

"She's trying to carry it on, while there's still time."

The man glanced at Anne, then back to the Doctor. It was obvious he had no thought of discussing important work with a girl. But Anne could not expect Dr. Brown to do all of her work for her.

"Mr. Bean, I have the paper my father was showing to leading business men along the Turnpike," she said. "He was going to ask you to read it. Your name was on his list. So I'll show it to you now. It's signed by Governor Mason."

She handed the paper to the tannery owner, gesturing to him to take it when he hesitated. He studied it for a long time, then scratched his head as he handed it back to Anne, pushing his big felt hat back as he did so. Iron gray hair he had. "A silver oak," Anne thought.

"I don't know if I rightly understand what the Guv'nor means," he said. "Do you?"

"Yes," Anne told him eagerly. "Papa was one of a group of business men who were asking delegates to meet in Ann Arbor on December 14th and reverse the decision of the September convention. This paper is authority from the Governor to do it."

"I've heard that September convention did wrong," Mr. Bean said, shoving his hat back down on his head. "Did your Paw say it was wrong?"

"Yes. We're losing the 5% commission on the sale of Federal lands because we're not a state," Anne said. "All states get it, but Michigan doesn't. We've got to give up the Ohio strip and ratify the Act of Congress and become a state."

Oakley Bean nodded and sucked his thin cheeks inward.

"Another thing," Anne went on, repeating what Franklin had told her to say. "President Jackson will leave office with a surplus in the Federal treasury. It's to be divided equally among the states, but Michigan won't get a share of that unless we're a state before he goes out."

The prospective delegate nodded again, but he looked at Dr. Brown instead of Anne.

"The committeemen — and Mr. Rogers was one of them — want seventy delegates to go to Ann Arbor and reverse the action taken in September. They must vote us to be a state right away, before Jackson leaves office," Dr. Brown said.

"That's the way you understand it, Doc?" Oakley Bean asked.

"That's the way I understand it," Dr. Brown assured him. "I've agreed to do as the young lady asks, and help her all I can."

"Can I put you down as a delegate to go, Mr. Bean?" Anne asked eagerly. "I mustn't do it unless you pledge to be there and vote to accept the Act of Congress."

"You kin put me down," he said, nodding deliberately.

"Maybe you'd see one or two of the men on Mr. Rogers' list," Dr. Brown suggested. "It's not easy for his daughter to cover all the ground. That's why I was helping her today."

Mr. Bean selected the names he would be responsible for.

"You kin put them down too," he said. "I'll vouch for 'em. They'll be there."

After that Anne wasn't afraid as they drove from grist mill to saw mill to Turnpike store. By nightfall most of the county had been accounted for, and all of the men Anne had talked with were pledged as delegates for Governor Mason.

"I was a little fearful when we started that you couldn't manage this task," Dr. Brown admitted to Anne as they drove back toward Hillsdale County. "Now I think you can. You stay the night with us and tomorrow I'll give you letters to some of the men I know who live farther out along the Turnpike. I've an idea they'll offer help too. More readily than if I was with you, mayhap."

It would save hours of driving if she did not return to the settlement that night, and Polly knew she might be away for several days. But there was no pleasure in the thought of seeing Mrs. Meager and Alice again.

"I'm afraid it would make your sister too much trouble," Anne told the Doctor.

"Now you pay no mind to Moll," he said with a chuckle. "You won't be the first person I've brought home for her to feed and put up for the night. Soon as you've had your supper you'll be ready for bed anyway."

Anne was ready for bed right then. Since daylight she had been driving in the sharp winter air. She would eat her supper and go to bed and have no more words with Mrs. Meager or Alice.

Dr. Brown wrote letters for Anne that night which served to take much of the load from her shoulders. The daughter of the Yankee peddler who had been killed before he could complete his mission was not left to carry on alone by the backwoodsmen on Papa's list as Anne learned. When she went home, it was with a grateful heart.

"Frost-Bitten Convention"

Driving the last miles home to the tavern with little 'y's' opposite all the names on her list, Anne's thoughts returned to Polly. By this time she should have heard from Eb. Perhaps she already would be packing her things, preparing for the trip back East. There would be all the work of getting her furniture hauled to Detroit, and of finding what to do with it until the lake boats were running again in the spring. Unless Eb had not written. Never once since Polly had been in Michigan had she heard from Eb, although she had let him know where she was situated. Perhaps he wouldn't write now. If he didn't — Anne's thoughts raced ahead. If he didn't send for her — If Polly were to stay in Michigan — .

Nothing was disturbed when she entered the tavern livingroom, and the question in her eyes was answered by a negative shake of Polly's head.

"I've had no word, Anne," she said, "But it's not for

myself I'm worried. It's for you. Mr. Watling has been here inquiring for you."

"Mr. Watling?" Anne gasped.

"Mr. Doyle tells me he's fearful that the sheriff may have got a look at your father's papers before he gave them to you. The sheriff didn't read them, Mr. Doyle is certain. But he had a glimpse of them."

"Are the sheriff and Mr. Watling friends?" Anne asked.

"Mr. Doyle says they're both Whigs."

"Oh," Anne groaned. "What did you say to Mr. Watling?"

"Fortunately, I didn't see him," Polly told her. "I don't know what I would have said, taken off guard that way. He came when I was out and the hired girl didn't know where you'd gone or when you'd be back."

Anne sighed with relief. "I think I know what to tell him," she said slowly. "If he comes again, I think I know what to say."

He came that evening to offer polite condolences and help, and to inquire of the plans Polly and Anne might be making. Polly assured him there was little they could plan, right then. She had not heard from her brother, who was in the shipping business in Boston.

"He may well be out of the country on a long voyage at this very time," she told him. "His business takes him around the world."

"And you, my dear child?" Mr. Watling said, addressing Anne. He was almost convincing.

"I'll be provided for, I know," Anne assured him. "My Aunt and Uncle have offered me a home with them on their farm near Ionia. I can go there. But this week I've been to see Dr. Brown and his sister, Mrs. Meager, on school business. They know Reverend Pierce and he's state superintendent of schools now."

"Oh," Mr. Watling said, and Anne thought there was a note of satisfaction in his voice. "You are the young lady who wanted to teach the school here at the settlement, aren't you?"

"Yes," Anne admitted. "I've never stopped being interested in teaching."

"Well, my dear child, if your friends shouldn't be able to help you — and that is possible — you come to me. A little later on, perhaps, I might be able to do something. Who knows? This is a changing world we live in."

Anne thanked him, and after he had again assured them of his kindly intentions he left, without asking more about Anne's absence from the tavern.

"But Anne, suppose he should go to Dr. Brown or Mrs. Meager?" Polly asked, after he had left.

"Dr. Brown wouldn't tell him why I was there or what I've been doing," Anne assured her. "He acted as a committeeman himself, until I got started. He's as deep in this as I am. And as for Mrs. Meager, that's what I told her I was there for. School business. That's exactly what I said."

Two days before the December convention Franklin returned to the tavern, bringing some of the delegates with him for the night. He was tired, but almost triumphant and he smiled with satisfaction when Anne relieved him of his heavy coat.

"If they all get to Ann Arbor, we're all right," he told Anne and Polly while they sat in the lamplight before the fireplace after the guests had retired. "They're all pledged and nothing but blizzards and accidents can keep them from action that should make us a state. I saw Dr. Brown, too, Anne," he added. "I know how well you carried out your part of the work."

Anne felt almost shy at his words of praise. It was pleasant indeed to know he thought she had done well.

Polly, too, seemed to share Anne's pleasure. She brought tart apples from the barrel in the cellar and they munched contentedly and in silence for a little time.

"Polly, would you and Anne like to drive to Ann Arbor with me?" Franklin asked unexpectedly. "You could ride back with Mr. Doyle. We couldn't attend the convention, of course, but we'd be there to know right off whether all went as planned."

Anne looked at Polly hopefully. How she did want to go!

"You haven't been away from the tavern since you came here," Franklin reminded Polly. "And as for Anne, she has a right to be there at the finish, it seems to me."

"She's earned that right, as you say, Franklin," Polly agreed. "There's little business at the tavern these winter months and I have good help. It might be just as well if I did get away for a day or two. We'll take Susan along, of course."

So before daylight, while the Whigs were still asleep,

they all drove quietly from the settlement. The morning of December 14th found them at the Inn in Ann Arbor, where delegates were assembling. Anne and Susan and Polly sat at their table in the diningroom, listening to the conversation around them, while Franklin mingled with the men, shaking hands and nodding agreement with the views that were being expressed.

These delegates would not haggle, Anne knew. Keen-minded men they were, and practical. They would accept the Act the United States Congress had passed, abandon the Ohio strip, and take the Upper Peninsula. These were not the men who had gathered three months earlier to wrangle and stubbornly vote to defy both Ohio and the national Congress.

"Jackson's got a few more weeks in office before he turns the government over to that Little Magician, Van Buren," Franklin said, after the last of the delegates had left for their meeting at the courthouse.

"But Jackson removed Governor Mason," Anne reminded him. "Can we depend on Jackson now?"

"I think so," Franklin replied. "He knows he let his own man down, because of Ohio's power. But the national election changed all that. Van Buren's another of Jackson's men and the Democrats will stay in the saddle. Jackson has nothing to fear from Ohio now. Lucius Lyon thinks this action we're taking here today will be accepted by Congress. Then Jackson will act in favor of Mason and Michigan before he leaves office."

"Could Lyon be wrong?" Susan suggested.

"Yes," Franklin admitted and his face became thoughtful. "We're sending a second group of delegates to Congress with a second decision. But it's the decision the Congress asked for, and it's all we can do now."

Waiting for the delegates to come back was a monotonous business. Franklin paced restlessly from window to window. He melted the frost that covered the window panes with the warmth of his hand, to clear little port holes through which he could watch the street. Certainly, Anne thought, Governor Mason had no follower more devoted than this young surveyor with the arresting dark skin and long, light hair. Now and then he would turn from his viewing station to smile nervously at the ladies, or to offer to get coffee for them. Then he would return to his vigil.

Anne found her mind wandering from the deliberations at the courthouse to think first of Franklin and then of Polly. Strange it was that Polly had no word from Eb. If she didn't hear — certainly Polly wouldn't want to go and live with Aunt Ellen and Uncle Luther. Not Polly, with her independent ways and her tavern full of furniture. What would Polly do? What was she thinking as she sat and waited, soberly, and saying little, to hear the outcome of the convention?

At last the men came back to the Inn. Mr. Doyle was beating his hands together and stomping his feet energetically.

"One little pot-bellied stove is all they've got to heat their courthouse," he grumbled. "Faith and was that a frost-bitten convention, as they're saying."

"But what did you do?" Franklin pressed him. "How was the action?"

" 'Twas unanimous, as planned, and what else did you expect?" Mr. Doyle replied. "Seventy-one delegates answered roll call. One more'n you'd set out to get. Now it's up to Mason to get our decision to Washington fast as he can, and up to Lyon and Crary to get it accepted."

CHAPTER 15

"J Sing a State"

> "I sing a state, of all the best,
>   Michigan, my Michigan.
> I sing a state with riches blest,
>   Michigan, my Michigan.
> Thy mines unmask a hidden store
>   But richer thy historic lore;
> More great the love thy builders bore
>   Michigan, my Michigan."

Through the sunless days of December and January, Anne found herself thinking more and more of Polly's brother Eb. Strange indeed that Polly had no word from him. Anne tried to recall everything that Nate had told her of Polly's marriage with her father, and the lawsuit that followed. Tried to recall all that Granny had said about Polly and her family. It didn't seem natural, somehow, that Eb wouldn't offer Polly a home now, when he had wanted above all to keep her from marrying Papa and going away.

More than once Anne was at the point of asking Polly outright what she thought, but something always stopped

—188—

her. Just when she was about to speak, the old tightness would come in her throat, or the hired girl would come in asking questions, or travellers would stop at the tavern. So the days passed, and neither Anne nor Polly mentioned Eb's name.

Nor did Polly talk to Anne at all about her plans. If Polly wasn't going back East, was she going to Ionia to live with Aunt Ellen? Aunt Ellen didn't have a big house like the tavern. What would be done with all of Polly's furniture and two more people, in the little log farm house Aunt Ellen had described to them? Polly would have thought of all that.

Could it be that she was intending to stay right here at the settlement, running the tavern, should Eb not send for her? Of a certainty she could manage if that was what she had set her mind to. Ever since spring when Uncle Luther and Aunt Ellen and Oscar left, it was Polly who had run the tavern, for Papa had been away more than he was home. If that was her plan — to stay in Michigan and run the tavern — there was an idea in Anne's mind. It kept coming back to her.

Anne wished for Nate. She could have talked to Nate. She thought of writing to him, or even of finding an excuse to make a trip to Kent County to see him, but while she was turning that idea over in her mind a storm swept down from the lakes, blocking the roads with great, uneven drifts and stopping all stage and coach travel. For days snow swirled through the sky, hiding even the woods across the clearing.

The day after the blizzard abated Baw Beese appeared,

bringing a shivering group of half-starved Indians with him.

"How," he said as he stood in the doorway. "Injun got message for Anne."

"A message?" Anne asked, scarcely expecting any very intelligible reply.

"Injuns cold. Injuns hungry," Baw Beese said. But he took an envelope from beneath his blanket as he spoke and held it grudgingly before her.

Anne did not ask for the envelope at once, although she was exceedingly curious about it. Who could have sent a letter to her by Baw Beese? She closed the heavy kitchen door against the bitter cold that had followed the snow, and motioned the Indians to the fireplace. Over the blazing logs an iron kettle of beans was simmering, and the rich aroma of salt pork filled the room. Anne knew the Indians would have to be fed, and if any guests stopped at the tavern that night, some other main dish would have to be provided for them. So she filled plates and did not ask for the message. When Baw Beese relinquished the envelope at last, Anne immediately recognized Nate's handwriting.

"Where did you get this, Baw Beese?" Anne asked.

The Indian motioned to one of the braves in his party; a young man Anne had seen many times before.

"He go north to big river before storm," Baw Beese said. "Pottawatomies told to go in spring, but Pottawatomies fear Iroquois on new reservation. Pottawatomies look for lands between lakes where no white man settle."

Anne knew the Indians had been told to go to a reservation west of the Mississippi when they ceded Nattawa-Seepe to the government. Doubtless some of the younger braves had been looking for a hunting ground safe from the white men, and had gone as far as the Grand River.

"And when he was north to the Big River, what happened?" Anne pressed, still holding the envelope in her hand and slowly breaking the seal.

"He see Nate. They talk. Nate send message back," Baw Beese explained, gesturing to the letter.

Anne opened it and read:

"My dear Cousin:

"Today I had a chance to send this message to you by one of Baw Beese's braves. It will reach you as soon by the Indian as by post and perhaps sooner.

"First let me say that all is well with me. I arrived safely back in Kent County as expected. Every day we work hard, all hands, for there are orders ahead for the fine furniture this little industry is turning out. A man has a right to be proud of such craftsmanship as is done here.

"But it is not of myself that I am writing. I am eager to know what has taken place with you. Maw writes that you have not yet come to live with them, and it must be because Polly has had no word from her brother Eb. If Polly should not hear from Eb, Paw and Maw would gladly give her a home with them, crowded as they would be.

"For you, though, I have a plan that should be welcome to all. There is a school here and the teacher is getting married soon. That means there will be no teacher in the spring. So I have made bold to speak to my employer about you, for he is the school moderator. He would like to talk to you. He knows that you did not go to Miss Willard's school, nor to any similar school, but I told him about Susan and that she is a good teacher. He thinks if you set your mind to it, and she helped you, you could be prepared well enough to teach this little country school when the present teacher marries.

"This would provide a way for everyone, Anne, and I would have a good feeling about having you here, where I could look out for you. So write and tell me what transpires with you and Polly, and what your judgment may be about this offer. Then I will talk again to the school moderator.

Truly your cousin,
Nate."

Anne blinked back tears of happiness as she read. Nate, always her best friend, still was looking out for her. Here was a real opportunity, too, if nothing better offered; if Polly did return East or, remaining in Michigan, chose the security of Uncle Luther's home to the scheme that Anne had been dreaming up.

Anne slipped the letter into her pocket. She need not answer it at once, but she would have to talk to Polly soon, so she would know how to reply.

The time came quicker than she anticipated. Late the next afternoon the stage coach stopped before their door. Polly was the first to see it.

"Anne! It's Eb!" Polly gasped.

There was no mistaking the look of dread on Polly's face, and when Anne peered through the speck of window pane that was not covered with frost, she felt instinctively that Polly had reason for alarm.

A huge man was plowing his way through the deep snow to the tavern steps, satchel in hand. He wore a black broadcloth coat, a high black hat, and Anne was sure his ears were stinging with cold, although a muffler was pushed up under his chin and around the back of his neck. His breath, freezing in the bitter air, billowed and puffed before him.

"He'll be in a state," Polly whispered. "That was no pleasant drive out from Detroit in this weather."

Polly opened the tavern door as Eb struggled the last steps through the snowbanks.

"Brother Eb," Polly said, extending her hand to him.

Brother Eb removed his hat and shook Polly's hand briefly, with no show of emotion.

"You must be frozen and very tired," Polly said closing the door behind him. "Let me take your things. This is my step-daughter, Anne Rogers."

Brother Eb bowed in Anne's direction, scarcely looking at her. He set his satchel down, took off his coat, and tugged at the heavy boots he wore while Polly nervously disposed of his things and tried to help.

"I'll get some hot coffee," Anne offered and started for the kitchen.

"You can get me some supper, if there's anything to eat in Michigan beside johnny cake and beans and dried apple pie," he said taking note of her for the first time. "That seems to be the general bill of fare here."

It was a statement of fact, so far as Eb was concerned. He was not exactly petulant. Disdainful, he seemed.

Anne observed every particular of Eb's well-groomed appearance as he relieved himself of his heavy outer clothing. He was taller than Papa had been, and square shouldered, and with too much stomach. But he was a man of great dignity and he carried his weight as though he were proud of it. His hair and beard were both coal black and trimmed short. His eyes were gray and lacking altogether in expression. Annoyed as she was sure he was, what with the snow and cold and the disagreeable trip, his face was a mask revealing no emotion.

"We can offer eggs and smoked ham and fried potatoes and dried corn," Polly suggested. "Or if you'd prefer, we have buckwheat cakes and sausage and maple syrup."

"I'll take the ham," Eb said briefly.

Anne started from the room to tell the hired girl to prepare the food, wondering as she did so how Eb would like his eggs, but she heard the first of his conversation with Polly.

"So you're a widow now. I should think the least you could have done was let your brother know."

Anne almost stopped in the doorway. What was Eb saying? That Polly hadn't let him know Papa was dead, that was what! How had he found out? Slowly she drew the door shut behind her, hoping to hear Polly's reply, but Polly did not answer. Instead, Eb's deep, resonant voice came to her.

"Not that I blame you for not being proud of it. Carrying out the bidding of that upstart Mason, as he was at the time. But you might have sent me word, instead of letting me find it out from a clerk who saved a newspaper until such time as I should get back to Boston."

So that was it! Polly had never written to Eb at all. Anne and Aunt Ellen had just assumed that she had done

-194-

it. And he had been away, as Polly had said he might well be.

Anne helped to prepare the meal, giving Polly time to be alone with her brother, but she was anxious to hear more of what Eb had to say.

During the dinner Polly attempted to visit cheerfully with Eb. She told him how mincemeat was prepared for the pie, how they obtained their food, and of the ample barrels of apples in the cellar and vegetables buried in sand. Eb's replies were monosyllables, but he ate with relish.

Polly had seated Eb where he could not have a view into the kitchen when the hired girl cleared away the food and brought in the pie. The Indians were still there, huddled on the floor near the warmth of the fireplace. They had eaten the beans and pork which Anne and Polly had expected to share with them that night. Eb, clearly, had no interest in the kitchen. As soon as he had finished the meal he chose the largest and most comfortable chair in the room and with a profound "Now," turned his attention to his sister and Anne.

"Tell me what steps you have taken to settle the estate," he said, addressing Polly. "Have you sold the peddler's business or the tavern yet?"

Sold the peddler's business! Or the tavern! Anne had not thought of such a thing. She looked at Polly and it seemed to her that her father's widow was bracing herself for this encounter. Polly was wearing a dark red wool dress and her hands, locked together in her lap, were all white knuckles. Her face, too, was white above the deep color of her dress, the muscles tight across her cheek bones.

"The only heirs he left were Anne and myself," Polly said, her voice low with nervousness. "We have not sold anything."

"Then I'll proceed to do so at once," Eb announced. "I would have placed the advertisements in the Detroit papers when I was there, had I known."

He glanced at Anne fleetingly. "I'll see that you get your fair and rightful share of everything," he said. "Have you relatives to go to?"

Anne's "yes" was little more than a whisper.

"The tavern should bring a good sum, and the peddler's business too, if he left a decent stock of goods," Eb went on. "You'll not go penniless, girl," he added with another nod in Anne's direction. Then he turned again to Polly.

"I don't see why you didn't take these steps long ago," he said. " 'Tis true you can't ship your goods back home until the lakes open in the spring. Was that what held you back? Was that your reason for taking no action?"

For a moment Polly hesitated, then she answered him.

"No, Eb. It was never my intention to sell the tavern unless Anne wanted her share. So far this winter we've made out fairly well. We've learned that we can manage this business."

Polly's voice came back to her as she spoke, and she seemed to have more confidence after she had answered, but her reply invoked immediate anger.

"Not sell the tavern! What are you thinking of? Of course you'll sell!"

He got to his feet and, scowling, walked nearer to the fireplace, turning his back toward the heat. He was a huge, menacing figure as he stood there, surveying the big room and the furniture which made it a place of rare distinction.

"Polly, I've had enough of your nonsense," he said sternly. "Look what you did. Stripped your own home of all its furnishings to drag them out here into this frozen backwoods tavern. Perhaps there was some slight excuse when you did it. You were a young girl, thinking you were in love. Now you're a defenseless widow woman, and I am head of the family. We'll have no more of that kind of stupid stubbornness. The estate must be settled and you'll come home with me."

Anne looked from Eb to Polly. There was no sign of weakness in her white face, no unclasping of the taut hands in her lap.

"This is my home, Eb," Polly replied. "This is where he brought me and here we had our home. Here I stay."

For a few seconds Eb stared at her, his mouth half open in surprise. Then his jaws clamped shut and he took a few steps toward his sister. Anne would not have been surprised to see him take her by the shoulders and shake her roughly, but he made no move to lay a hand on her.

"Is there a lawyer in this settlement?" he demanded. "There must be courts, even out here. You'll find that a court will decide estates have to be settled. This one is going to be, my fine lady. Your furniture comes back East with you, and the girl gets her fair share of everything else. Is that understood?"

Polly did not answer.

"Furthermore, I have no intention of spending days out here taking care of the business. Is there a lawyer in the settlement?"

"There is none," Polly replied.

"Then tomorrow I drive back to Jonesville and see where one is to be found. Tomorrow each of you will start packing your personal belongings." He looked at Anne again. "Where do your relatives live?"

Anne thought the one word would choke her. "Ionia," she replied.

Ionia might have been as far away as Chicago for all Eb knew or cared.

"Send word to them by the next post that you are coming," he ordered her. "Let them know that you will have your share of your father's estate soon, and that within a week you will be ready to make the move. A week is as much time as I can spare, managing this business."

Polly spoke up then.

"Eb, I think Anne has the right to decide for herself whether she wants to go to Ionia to her relatives, or stay here in the home her father left to us," Polly said stoutly. "For myself, I have no intention of leaving it, now that I know I can make a go of the business. That I have learned, these past three months. That Anne knows too, by now."

Anne wanted to rush to Polly's side. She wanted to clasp her arms about those narrow shoulders, pressed so rigidly against the back of the rocker in which Polly sat. But any show of emotion would be a show of weakness in Eb's eyes, she felt certain, so she sat as straight in her own chair as Polly was sitting, her hands like ice and her throat tight. Finally she found her voice.

"I had no thought of leaving the tavern," Anne said to Eb deliberately. "Polly and I have made out well together."

There had been another vague thought in her mind, but it was gone now. She would stay at the tavern just so long as Polly stayed.

Eb drew a long breath. Then he turned and faced Anne.

"How old are you, young lady?"

"Seventeen next month," Anne answered.

"You are still a minor. Go to your room."

At first Anne did not obey. Polly needed her, she was certain. How could she leave Polly alone, at the mercy of Eb? But when she hesitated he turned on her like thunder.

"There are personal matters I have to discuss with my sister," Eb fairly shouted. "Go to your room, and at once!"

Anne gave one last look at Polly. Unless Polly told her to stay, she would have to go. Polly moved her head ever so slightly toward the stairway and tried to smile.

"There are things we have to say to each other, Anne," Polly said and then Anne knew she must go. Without a word to Eb, or another glance in his direction, she slowly climbed the stairs. As soon as Polly came to her room, Anne would go to her. Whatever Polly had in mind to do, Anne would be with her.

But Polly did not come upstairs. The log burned low

and at last Anne grew drowsy, and the shadow of the poster bed with its ruffled canopy wavered against the far wall as her eyelids drooped. To her half-consciousness there came the sound of a creaking door. What was that sound? She had heard it before. It was very familiar.

Anne sat up with a start. Had she really heard the grating of the door to the shed where the wagons were kept? Papa's peddler's wagon. Nate's old sleigh. She listened and heard nothing. But the sound had been very real. Puzzled, she went to the window and peered out into the tavern yard below.

In the weak light of the cloud-covered moon Anne could make out the forms of two horses. As her eyes adjusted to the dimness, she saw that the shed door was indeed open, and she made out the figure of Baw Beese clumsily harnessing the horses. Then she saw Polly, standing in the entrance to the shed.

Anne was wide awake now and running downstairs. From its peg in the kitchen she grabbed her coat, pulled her knitted cap from the sleeve where she always put it, and shoved it down over her head as she ran out into the back yard. The snow in the path was beaten hard and she knew she would not sink in over her shoetops, so she wasted no time in putting on her boots.

The light from the opened kitchen door had stopped both Polly and Baw Beese. They waited in the shadow of the buildings until she reached them.

"What are you doing? Where are you going?" Anne asked breathlessly. Polly stepped back into the dark shed and Anne followed her.

"Polly, what are you doing?" Anne repeated.

"I've got to go, Anne," Polly said and her voice was scarcely audible. "I've got to get a lawyer, and Uncle Luther too. Baw Beese will go as far as Marshall with me, then he'll go on to Ionia."

"You mean —" Anne hesitated. "Can a lawyer stop Eb? What is he going to do?"

"He's going to put everything up for sale, as he said," Polly told her. "Right away. Tomorrow. He's determined to take me back to Boston with him. There's a lawyer in Marshall. If I had a lawyer I'd know my rights."

Indignation mounted as the full meaning of Polly's words came to her.

"He can't do that!" she insisted. "The tavern's half mine. He said it himself. What right has he?"

"You're a minor and we're both females," Polly answered. "Maybe he can. I don't know the law, and he'll do it in spite of everything if I don't find a way to stop him. Hush! Is that a rig turning into the yard?"

"Yes," Anne whispered. "Somebody's driving in. I'll put them up for the night so you can go on. We do need a lawyer. But it'll take most a week to get Uncle Luther down here from Ionia. Polly, what were you intending to do? I heard what Eb said this afternoon about your not writing to him. What were you planning to do?"

Polly's breath came sharply and she did not answer at once.

"Tell me. Before they get here and we can't talk," Anne urged.

"I was going to stay right here where your father

brought me," Polly whispered. "I was going to carry on with his tavern business and I was hoping — "

"What?" Anne urged. They're almost here!"

"I was hoping I could get enough together to carry out his plan and send you to Miss Willard's school, Anne. I hadn't thought about selling the peddler's business though. With that money perhaps I could do it. I should have thought of it."

Anne thought she couldn't breathe at all. She opened her lips, but no words came. In the darkness she reached for Polly's hand and as she gripped it, the rig drew to a halt and a man jumped from the sleigh into the snow.

"Franklin!" Polly and Anne said in the same breath.

"Hello!" Franklin called out cheerfully. "What are you two doing out here?"

"Hush!" Anne whispered, but the warning came too late. Another minute and the kitchen door opened, revealing Eb in night attire, his overcoat draped about his shoulders.

"Polly!" Eb called sharply. "What's going on out there?"

"Who's that?" Franklin asked, staring at Eb's great figure silhouetted in the kitchen door.

"It's Polly's brother Eb," Anne answered. "He's come to take her to Boston and she doesn't want to go."

"Then why should you?" Franklin asked, turning to Polly who was half hidden in the shadows within the shed.

"Polly, do you hear me?" Eb's voice rang out in the sharp night air. "Come to the house this minute!"

Eb had his heavy boots in his hand. While Polly and

Franklin and Anne watched, he leaned over and began pulling them on over his bare feet. Plainly he was coming to the shed.

"Polly was going to Marshall to get a lawyer," Anne whispered. "She was going to send Baw Beese on to Ionia for Uncle Luther. Eb's going to sell everything we've got and take Polly back with him."

"He can't do that against Polly's will," Franklin said, then turning to her he added, "We've got laws in Michigan to protect property rights, Polly. I don't know the law, of course, but he can't force you to do what's against your will."

"He'll stop me from going to Marshall now," Polly answered. "And I can't stand up against Eb. Not alone."

She shuddered as she said it and Anne was sure it was true.

"We do need a lawyer, Franklin," Anne said. "Baw Beese, why can't you take the rig and go? You know the way. Have the lawyer come to us tomorrow, then drive on for Uncle Luther. You'll do it for us, won't you?"

Baw Beese, who had been standing close to the horses, his hands stroking their warm bodies, grunted in assent.

"You two go into the house before Eb drags you in," Franklin said to Anne and Polly. "I'll get Baw Beese started with the message, then I'll come in."

Eb, meantime had started down the steps and out into the snow-filled yard.

"He'll get snow in his shoes," Polly whispered. "He'll catch cold —. We're coming, Eb," she called.

It was difficult for Anne to understand why Polly should

care if Eb froze to death. She glanced at Polly as they started toward the kitchen. Again she had Papa's old fur cap pulled down over her ears and his worn gray muffler about her neck.

"What'll we say?" Polly asked as she hurried along beside Anne.

There was little time to think of what to say. Already Eb loomed before them, ready to herd them back into the tavern.

"What were you two doing?" he demanded.

"A rig drove into the tavern yard," Anne replied. "We had to find out whether it was a tavern guest or who it was."

Eb did not reply.

"It turned out to be a friend of the family who has come out from Detroit," Polly told him. "A Franklin Williams. You'll meet him right soon, Eb."

It was clear that Eb was not convinced as they stumbled back into the tavern kitchen. He stopped long enough to give one disgusted glance at the Indians, rolled in their blankets near the huge fireplace, and walked through to the big room, Anne and Polly behind him.

"A fine situation I find you in, Polly," he said as he stood before the fireplace and looked down at her. "Now I want to know what you were up to, just now."

As Anne looked at Eb, his long night shirt hanging below his overcoat, his hair in disarray and his thick, wrinkled neck without the protection of a collar, he suddenly became much less frightening. But Polly, speechless, sat down in the chair nearest the kitchen door and started to pull off her boots, and did not reply.

"Answer me!" Eb insisted. "What were you doing?"

"I'll tell you," Anne spoke up, a little surprised at her own boldness. "Polly and I don't altogether like your plan for selling our tavern and all. We've sent for my Uncle Luther and a lawyer."

Eb stared down at Anne as though he had not heard aright. Then he turned his back on her and faced Polly.

"Is this true?" he demanded.

Polly nodded, and at last her voice came back to her. For all her strength and courage, plainly Polly was afraid of Eb.

"It's true, Eb," she admitted, her voice scarcely audible. "I don't think I should be forced against my will to leave my own home."

"So you're sending for Uncle Luther, whoever he may be, instead of listening to your own brother," Eb fairly shouted at Polly. "Am I not head of this family and responsible for you now? You disregarded my judgment once before, and look where it got you. Your own home! A tavern in this wilderness with a kitchen full of foul-smelling Indians. Is this where you want to spend the rest of your days?"

"Yes," Polly said and her face became as set as Eb's own. "I can earn my way here well enough, Eb. I have no wish to be beholding to anyone."

Before Eb could say more Franklin came in, stomping the snow off his feet and removing his boots in the kitchen.

He entered the big room of the tavern, smiling cheerfully. Polly introduced him to Eb.

"I have wonderful news for you," he said as though he knew nothing of what had been taking place at the tavern. "Have you any cider, Mrs. Rogers? We should propose a toast tonight. A toast to the State of Michigan!"

"The State of Michigan?" Anne repeated.

"Yes," Franklin answered. "Congress accepted the action of the delegates in Ann Arbor last December without a question. Jackson signed the bill admitting us as the twenty-sixth state on the twenty-sixth of January, this year 1837. Mason is officially governor of Michigan and all's well!"

"So you've bullied your way into the Union at last," Eb said. "A fine spectacle this has been! A national disgrace!"

"We've been admitted, as we had a right to be long ago," Franklin said, looking Eb squarely in the face. "A fine spectacle, I'll agree. Of attempted injustice in high places."

"And now that you're a state, what now?" Eb asked and the tone of his voice made Anne fearful that there was something beneath the question. "It seems to me I've read something of Mason's plans for Michigan."

"He has plans indeed," Franklin said proudly. "For improved schools, improved roads, locks at the Straits of Mackinac, and railroads."

"And railroads," Eb repeated mockingly. "That's what I understood. A railroad that will run from Detroit all the way to St. Joseph. Isn't that what I read in the Detroit papers while I was waiting to get out to this . . . this inn?"

"Doubtless you did. It's part of the Governor's plan," Franklin agreed, but Eb was turning back to face Polly.

"A railroad from Detroit to St. Joseph," he repeated. "What, my dear sister, do you think that is going to do to your tavern business here on the Turnpike?"

Eb's question silenced everyone. A railroad to St. Joseph would indeed put an end to most of the stage coach and wagon travel across the state. It might well put an end to the business Polly had hoped to continue.

"Now will you listen to reason, Polly?" Eb continued. "Believe me, I didn't make this awful trip for any purpose but your own good. You had your own way once. Can't you see what will happen in another year or two if you don't listen to me now? You'll have no business at all, and I'll just have this to do all over again."

Polly looked at Eb and then at Franklin, but to this latest argument even Franklin had no answer. Mason did indeed have plans for great improvements in the state, and the railroad would work to Polly's disadvantage. What would she do if there was no business at the tavern? There was no mistaking the look of despair that came over her face.

But the plan that Anne had been thinking of! Mason's railroads wouldn't affect that. If Polly did indeed want to stay in Michigan and manage the tavern, and send Anne to Miss Willard's school as she had said —

"Polly, that well may happen," Anne spoke up. "But if you can run this tavern here on the Turnpike, why couldn't you run a tavern in Detroit?"

Polly looked at Anne in surprise. "In Detroit?" she repeated.

"Yes, Detroit," Anne said. "Where there are lyceums and concerts and churches, and ladies' clubs that Franklin's mother could take you to."

Polly rose from her chair quickly and looked from Anne to Franklin.

"We could do it, Polly," Anne urged, and Franklin echoed her words.

"You certainly could," he said confidently. "Mother'll help you, and Susan too. Now that Mason's won and I can put my mind back to my business, I want Susan home again. What is there to stop you?"

"Nothing," Anne said with assurance. "Nothing, if Polly's willing. The laws of Michigan will protect our rights. We'll have our lawyer here tomorrow."

Polly did not look at Eb, who stood like a monument beside the massive highboy, his great coat still draped over his shoulders. But there wasn't any question of what she would do now. Once more she was ready to defy Eb to the end.

"There's cider in the cellar, Franklin," Polly said. "And fresh venison Baw Beese brought back from the woods this evening. It's late, but we should celebrate the news you've brought us this night. We should frame a fitting toast to the new State of Michigan."

"Two toasts," Anne said, stepping to Polly's side. "One to the new state and one to the new tavern. Rogers' Tavern in Detroit, where the Turnpike and the railroad both start!"

CHAPTER 16

A Time for Planning

Eb was defeated. Tomorrow the lawyer would be there from Marshall to tell Polly and Anne their rights. Before the end of the week Uncle Luther would come. Tonight they had Franklin and the glorious news of statehood and final victory. While Anne and Polly went to the kitchen for cider and sweet cakes and apples, and Franklin piled fresh logs on the fireplace, Eb climbed the stairs and went to bed.

The logs smouldered and crackled, then flared up into dancing red and golden flames while they sat before the fireplace and planned for tomorrow. Everybody at the settlement must know the news as fast as they could spread the word. Franklin would go first for Susan, stopping at every house on the way. Anne would go to Mr. Doyle's. Polly would arrange for a big feast at the tavern. Baw Beese had brought wild turkeys that night, and there was frozen venison hanging from beneath the eaves outside.

The women would bring pans of baked beans and johnny cake and vegetables from their cellars. There would be pies and cakes and cookies, made from old favorite recipes. Everyone in the settlement would be invited to come to the tavern tomorrow.

"Then will be the time to tell people you are prepared to sell all but the furniture," Franklin advised Polly. "The news will spread, and you and Anne will have no trouble selling all you wish to sell."

"It may be hard to find a place in Detroit where we can set up a new tavern," Polly suggested. "Do you think this is a move we can truly make, Franklin?"

"Detroit has been growing daily," Franklin assured her. "The news of our statehood will start a new wave of emigration in the spring, and more taverns will be needed. There was building going on all along Woodward Avenue, and on Woodbridge and Jefferson and Randolph streets last summer and fall. But if no suitable place is for sale, or prices are too high, there are ample building supplies to be had."

"Tonight is no time to figure about whether to buy or to build," Polly said. "We know too little tonight. There is too much to plan for tomorrow."

So Polly planned, and finally gave up planning and went to bed, leaving Anne and Franklin sitting before the smouldering logs in the cedar-scented warmth of the big room. The firelight shone on polished wood and brass. It caught up the yellow threads in the red plaid dress Anne wore and the gold in Franklin's hair. It reflected in the glass of the unlighted lamps, and there was a comforting sense of something settled and accomplished in the atmosphere.

"Now tell me about your plans, Franklin," Anne suggested. "With Mason safely in office and Michigan ready to expand as planned, what about you?"

"At last I shall do what should have been done two years ago." Franklin told her. "I finished my surveying course and was ready to follow my father in business when unfortunate things began to happen. The Ohio War and Mason's removal from office. I've done little these past two years but work with others who believed in Mason's program for building a great state. Now I must make up for lost time. Others have forged ahead while I did the work you know about so well."

Anne had not thought about that seriously, although once Susan had hinted at it. She had thought very little about how Franklin earned a living, or what he was doing when he was not carrying out one mission or another for the Governor.

"Other surveyors, of course," Anne said as the picture became clear to her. "They have set up offices and gotten the business."

Franklin nodded. "There are a good many surveying firms established in Detroit now, and it's true they have been getting the business. It would have gone hard with me, Anne, had Mason lost."

"But now that he has won?"

"All the men who have been working for Mason will help me get started, I know," Franklin assured her. "Crary and Reverend Pierce and Lucius Lyon. Lyon has been a surveyor, you remember. They are men who are known and their word carries weight. I'll open an office either in the capitol city or nearer where there's land needing to be surveyed, and give my full time and attention to it now."

"Perhaps not in the capitol city?" Anne asked, trying to keep the concern out of her voice. Part of the joy of her own plan to live in Detroit had been the thought that Franklin would be there too. It was hard to hide her feelings, but she went on quickly. "I hadn't thought much about your business, I confess. Every time I've seen you, you've been so absorbed in the work you were carrying on that I didn't question how you were making out otherwise."

"Others did, I'm afraid," Franklin told her. "I'm not altogether sure my father approved of letting Susan come out here to teach the settlement school when she might have remained at home, had I been a good provider."

For a moment Anne did not answer him. There had been another reason why Susan's venture into the settlement had been questioned, and well Anne knew it. Perhaps now was the time to talk about it at last, painful as the subject was. She stared into the fire, then drew a long breath.

"Not only your father," she said. "The Kirklands at the Female Seminary and Reverend Pierce, too, were reluctant to have her come here at first. I know, Franklin. I know what was said."

He did not reply, but got up and taking the tongs pushed carefully at the logs.

"You, too," Anne went on. "When I heard what Alice Meager had told, I was surprised that you gave your consent for Susan to come here."

He stood before the fireplace looking down at her.

"It was a disturbing story," he admitted. "Until the day I saw you at the races, I didn't know what to think about it. Susan was sure all along. She kept insisting that Alice was too weak and undecided a person to know how to cope with even a minor emergency. She wrote and told us what Mr. Doyle said had happened, after she came out here, too. But until that afternoon. . . ."

The afternoon of the races had been a disturbing memory too, and Anne flushed at the mention of it. But what was Franklin saying now? What did he mean? She must know.

"What did you think that afternoon, Franklin?" Anne finally asked, trying to keep her voice low and without the quaver she felt inside.

"When I saw you jump into the breach for Nate, without a thought for yourself, I was sure I knew just what had happened at the school," Franklin told her. "There was an emergency—a tragedy, it turned out to be—and I could see you doing the same thing then. Acting fast to find the best solution, without thought to the consequences for yourself. Isn't that about what happened, Anne?"

Anne felt as though the world was rolling off her shoulders. Franklin hadn't criticized her at the races as she and Nate both had thought. Franklin had understood. He had understood what she had done at the settlement school, too, without ever hearing her side of the story.

"There wasn't any time to think," she managed to say. "Not in either case. Something had to be done."

"And both times you acted rightly, it seemed to me," Franklin said coming back to sit beside her again. "I admired you for it, Anne. I was glad Susan was out here at the settlement after I'd met you. I never had a worry about her, after that."

Anne tried not to show the relief she felt.

"I'm glad you thought as you did," she told him. "I don't believe Susan's minded being out here, so far from the gaiety of the capitol city. I think she's been happy."

"She was satisfied because her heart was back East at Columbia's School of Medicine," Franklin replied. "This has been as good a place as any to wait out the time until a certain young man returns to Detroit and hangs out his shingle as a physician."

"I had thought that, too," Anne said softly. "She never really said so, though."

"She'll say what's on her mind and in her heart when the time comes," Franklin said. "I've known, though. But now enough about Susan and me. What about you, Anne? What are your plans for these next months just ahead?"

It was the first time he had ever asked Anne about her plans. They had never talked quietly about themselves, alone together, before. Anne felt no hesitancy about speaking freely, now.

"Nate has found a school in Kent County which he thinks I could teach in the spring," Anne told him. "If

Polly had gone back East with Eb, I'd have gone to live with Aunt Ellen and Uncle Luther, and tried to get the school. Nate thought Susan could help me well enough, so I'd be prepared. It's one plan that has developed."

He turned toward her quickly, a puzzled, questioning look on his face.

"You wouldn't leave Polly now?" he asked.

"No, I'd not leave Polly now," Anne hastened to assure him. "This move to Detroit was something I'd been thinking about for a long time before I mentioned it tonight. For months I've known I couldn't go to Miss Willard's School, but I kept thinking that if Polly were to stay here in Michigan we could live in Detroit. I could go to the Seminary where Susan went, and Polly could have something more like the life she enjoyed back East."

Franklin nodded and a pleased look came over his face. "It's a good school, and in no time at all they could prepare you to teach," he said.

"Will you assure Polly of that tomorrow?" Anne asked him. "She still has it in her mind that I should go to Miss Willard's School. She thinks with the money from Papa's peddler's business she can send me, but I'm fearful she'll need that and all we can get from the tavern too, to get established in Detroit. She'll need me to help her at first, too."

"She surely will," Franklin agreed, "but once she gets started, she can manage more easily than out here at the settlement. All she needs will be right there, in the stores around her. Then when you've taken your course at the

Seminary, you can teach for a little time, as you've planned. It would be too bad for you not to realize that ambition. You've cherished it for so long."

"Almost since the first day I came to Michigan," Anne told him.

"Will Nate mind?" Franklin asked. "This plan he had for you to be in Kent County, near him. You'll have to give that up. How will he feel about that?"

"Nate will understand," Anne assured him. "He'll be glad when he hears about Eb, and Polly's sure future here. Especially with you to help her get established in the right place in Detroit. Long ago Nate said he was sure Polly would have liked to stay in Detroit where there are advantages and refinements such as she was accustomed to. No, we need have no fear about Nate taking offense at anything we've worked out here tonight. He was only trying to look out for me, the best he could, when he told me about the school in Kent County."

"That's what I'd expect of Nate," Franklin said. "I've admired him greatly."

He reached over and took Anne's two hands in his then, and smiled as he looked into her eyes. "Now I'll look out for you, if you'll let me," he said softly. "Not that you need much looking out for. You're the bravest girl I ever knew, Anne, but if you ever do, I'll be there."

Anne knew in her heart that he would be. Whether his office was in the capitol city where she was going now, or somewhere else in this great new state, Franklin would be with her, steadfast and understanding. That was all she needed.